ABOUT THE EDITOR

STEPHEN ELLIOTT is a former stripper and the author of six books, including *Happy Baby,* a finalist for the New York Public Library's Young Lion Award, as well as a Best Book of 2004 in Salon.com, *Newsday, Chicago New City,* the *Journal News,* and the *Village Voice.* In addition to writing fiction, he frequently writes on politics. In 2004 he wrote a book about the quest for the Democratic presidential nomination titled *Looking Forward to It.* His most recent book is an almost all-true sexual memoir called *My Girlfriend Comes to the City and Beats Me Up.*

Elliott's writing has been featured in *Esquire,* the *New York Times, GQ, The Best American Nonrequired Reading, The Best American Erotica,* and *Best Sex Writing 2006.* He was a Wallace Stegner Fellow at Stanford University, and he is a member of the San Francisco Writers' Grotto. He is also the founder of the Progressive Reading Series, which helps authors raise money for and participate on behalf of progressive candidates across the country.

SEX
FOR
AMERICA

SEX
FOR
AMERICA

Politically Inspired Erotica

Edited by Stephen Elliott

HARPER ● PERENNIAL

NEW YORK ● LONDON ● TORONTO ● SYDNEY

HARPER ● PERENNIAL

HarperCollins books may be purchased for educational, business, or sales promotional use. For information please write: Special Markets Department, Harper-Collins Publishers, 10 East 53rd Street, New York, NY 10022.

FIRST EDITION

Designed by Justin Dodd

Library of Congress Cataloging-in-Publication Data

Sex for America : politically inspired erotica / edited by Stephen Elliott.—1st Harper Perennial ed.
    p. cm.
  ISBN: 978-0-06-135121-1
  1. Erotic stories, American. 2. American fiction—21st century.
I. Elliott, Stephen.
PS648.E7S483 2008
813'.01083538—dc22   2007041324

08 09 10 11 12 ID/RRD 10 9 8 7 6 5 4 3 2 1

CONTENTS

INTRODUCTION

The war on sex begins, most likely, with a blow job in the Oval Office. Monica's stained dress. The right's squealish protest, it's not about a blow job, it's about lying under oath. Ken Starr's decision to release the report, a giant mass of political porn uploaded and downloaded to the World Wide Web.

It's been seven years since the George W. Bush administration moved into the White House following a disputed election decided by the Supreme Court. George W. Bush would win two elections as the anti-sex candidate. He would fulfill his promise—lobbying for a constitutional ban on gay marriage, funding abstinence education across America, keeping condoms out of the classroom, packing the courts in preparation for an offensive on

Roe v. Wade. Meanwhile, an anti-obscenity squad is formed in the FBI. Resources are pulled from the war on terror and diverted to porn patrol. So while the administration is practicing torture on our behalf all over the world, websites depicting consensual S&M are being shut down at home.

In 2004, gay marriage was a crucial issue on many state ballots. The administration sided heavily with the forces against gay marriage. Meanwhile, the vice president's own daughter was gay. Now you can read Jerry Stahl's story of his own affair with Dick Cheney, which took place in the back of a gun store in Wyoming.

There is something profoundly sexual about campaigning for office. I've worked on campaigns where the tension was so tight, the hours so long, that passion was the only release. Every two years, marriages across the country are destroyed by the pressures of campaign season. This tension formed the starting point for James Frey's story, "The Candidate's Wife."

And it's not just the campaigns. We eroticize our political leaders. Something about being on the stage, wielding power. They smile at us. They represent our parents and our most base desires and provide targets for our anger. They betray us all the time, and we feel their abandonment, and this, too, needs release. In Charlie Anders's "Transfixed, Helpless, and Out of Control: Election Night 2004," we meet a young liberal, devastated by the election returns, surrendering control to a woman she's just met.

One purpose of fiction has always been to show a deeper truth than can be arrived at through journalism. In fiction we can examine an emotional truth, explore our interior selves. Like Michelle Tea, whose protagonist, a lesbian returned home to Florida, has sex with an old friend because he has joined the military and will be leaving in the morning for Iraq.

It would be fine to keep sex private, something behind closed doors. Unfortunately, when that happens, the politicians read that as a lack of public support. So now it's okay to block sex-ed materials, to outlaw practices arbitrarily judged obscene. Straight, gay, or kinky, to keep our freedoms, we have to be out of the closets.

In 2008 we're going to be given a chance to vote on what kind of control over our bodies we want the government to have. We're going to choose between candidates who believe in honest sex education and abstinence education. Those who believe in equal rights for gays and lesbians and those who believe sex between consenting adults is a sin.

The arts, of course, are on the front line of every cultural war. In this collection, I present you with twenty-four original stories by some of the best writers of our generation. These patriotic men and women are out of the closet having Sex for America.

—STEPHEN ELLIOTT

LI'L DICKENS

JERRY STAHL

I did not mean to sodomize Dick Cheney.

I mean, I'm not even gay. Or not usually. But when, to my surprise, I bumped into him—literally—at the counter of Heimler's Guns and Ammo, in Caspar, something clicked. And I'm not talking about the safety on my Mauser.

You see, there's another side to "Li'l Dickens," as the VP liked to refer to himself. Or, at least, a certain part of himself. *En privato.* He's tender. He's funny. He's pink. And he's a gun man, just like me.

But there I go, getting ahead of myself. . . . See, I was in Wyoming to pick up some German pistols. Not, you know, that I'm some kind of Nazi gun freak. Not even close. I just like the workmanship. The craft. A taste, as it happens, shared by Mr. Cheney.

"Schnellfeuerpistole," he smiled, eyes aglow as he surveyed the weapon.

"Model 1912," I smiled back. "Recoil, single-action."

"May I?"

He held out his hand. I had yet to recognize him. In his black-and-red hunting cap, flaps down, he could have been any pudgy hunter. Some sneering Elmer Fudd. But his nails were beautiful. Buffed as a showroom Bentley. I slapped the gun into his palm, butt first. "Good heft." His lips parted—fleshy magenta outside, meat-red within. "What are we looking at, ten inches?"

"Eleven."

The VP licked his lips and let out a trademark grunt. "Mmm . . . Barrel?"

"Five-and-a-quarter."

"Pocket-size. Nice."

"Looks can be deceiving." Our eyes met through his bifocals and I felt a shiver. "Short-bolt travel makes the rate of fire astronomical. But there's no control."

My new friend gave a little laugh that sounded like *hug-hug-hug.* "Believe it or not, I lose control myself."

"Really?"

Suddenly I had feelings I couldn't name. We'd drifted to the back of the store—no more than a counter, really, flanked by locked rows of guns on the wall and a signed photo of George Bush, Jr., in his flight suit, helmet under his arm, eyes triumphant, basket padded. His "Mission Accomplished" moment.

At some point the owner, a scruffy fellow who looked like Wilfred Brimley, had slung a Back in Ten sign in the window and disappeared. Maybe my future lovemate had given him a signal.

"Gee," I heard myself say, "you look a lot like—"

"I am," he said, "but you can call me . . . Dick."

He held open a door to the backroom. Which turned out to be more than that. My eyes took it in—sturdy mahogany desk and chairs, the portrait of J. Edgar Hoover over the crackling fire, the shelves stacked with sheaves of documents, busts of Lincoln, Jefferson and Julius Caesar and finally, as my eyes adjusted to the dark, the single bed in the corner. Rough green blanket tucked sharply under the mattress in military corners.

"Spartan," he growled. "A man in my position can't afford to be soft. We are, after all, at war."

"Wait? Is this the bunker?"

"Negative. The Veepeock is technically in the White House basement. Everybody knows it. That's the problem."

"Veepeock. I'm not sure I—"

"VPEOC." He cut me off, clearly a fellow used to getting his way. "White House terminology. Short for Vice Presidential Emergency Operations Center. You didn't think the bunker was in Washington, did you? That place is a cesspool of acronyms."

"But shouldn't there be security? Surveillance? Cameras?"

"Sometimes you don't want anybody looking." *Hug-hug-hug.* He tapped the cot. "Come on over here, soldier."

"Okay." Jesus. . .

In spite of myself, I drifted toward him. The man had tremendous animal magnetism. A musky aura of power seemed to emanate from his scalp. But, still . . . Shouldn't there be pull-down wall maps? Advisors? Data banks? A red phone with a key in it: hotline to Moscow . . . or Baghdad? Or Crawford?

I had, I realized, conflated Cheney's love nest with the president's war room in *Dr. Strangelove*. But I wasn't hobnobbing with Peter Sellers. Instead, here I was rubbing cheek to grizzled cheek with the real vice president, arguably the most powerful man in the free world. Freakish but true. While I stood there, frozen with fear, he sidled over and licked my face.

"Did you just lick me?"

My breath, as they say, came in short pants.

Cheney chuckled, ignoring my question, and swept his arm before him, indicating his little patch of heaven.

"I like a barracks feel. It's more Spartan. More . . . manly."

"But you didn't actually serve, did you? What was it, five deferments? You dropped out of Yale, then went to community college 'cause of the draft. I heard your wife even had a baby nine months to the day after they ended the childless married deferments."

His face reddened. A tiny wormlet of vein began to throb at his left temple. For one bad moment I thought he was either going to kill me or stroke out on the spot. Instead, he began to hug-chuckle all over again. "That Lynne. Bent her over the sink and slipped her the Dickens. Out came l'il Mary, right on time. My daughter's good people. Even if she is gay as Tallulah Bankhead's fanny."

With that he gave me another smooch. I wanted to recoil. And yet . . . I couldn't fight it. There was no other way. I had to ask.

"Are you gay, Mr. Vice President?"

"Me?" He leapt from the cot and ripped off his flannel with such ferocity I feared he might tear a ligament. "I had so many chicks in high school they used to call them Cheney-acs." Before this, I admit, I never knew the meaning of the word *swoon*. I couldn't help but stare at his tufted belly roll, his hairless chest, and—be still my heart—his pacemaker. Yes and yes again!

Embedded under the skin over his left nipple was the outline of what looked like a pack of Luckies.

He saw me ogling and beckoned. "Wanna touch?"

I nodded.

"Figured you might."

Slowly, I raised my fingers to his subcutaneous square. "It's . . . It's so *hard*."

What can I say? He was overweight, and grunting, and no doubt capable of having me disappeared with a single phone call. But, God, he was sexy. Soon my tentative touches turned to stroking, my stroking to outright caresses. Our eyes locked.

With that, it was on. Lynne's hubby yanked off his belt, let his pants drop around the tops of his waders, and popped his thumbs under the elastic of his white undies, which rode so high on his belly they covered the button. "Big-girl panties!"

Then he turned, waggling his ample bottom, and dropped to his hands and knees beside the army cot. I wasn't sure how to react, but before I could, he grunted, stretched, and pulled out a monkey-head bong.

"Who does this remind you of?"

It's all a little foggy after that. Yes, he reached in my pants and chuckled that he'd found the weapon of mass destruction. Yes, he wanted me to duct-tape the cheeks of his buttocks. Yes, he wanted me to spank and penetrate him and call his organ "Bunker Buster." The problem is I've never really been that into grass. It always hits me harder than anybody else. And there are blank spots. Which is just as well, since, even now, my gorge rises at the very notion of anal sex with an aging fat man who voted against Martin Luther King Day.

After our "encounter," he rolled off and, to my surprise, began to recite, in that trademark Oval Office–adjacent growl, albeit a tad slurry after the high-grade government Kkush:

> I saw the best minds of my generation destroyed by madness,
> > starving hysterical naked,
> Dragging themselves through the negro streets at dawn,
> looking for an angry fix.

After meeting the vice president, touching his pacemaker, and pounding him with a savagery that still makes me cringe, I did not think anything could surprise me. But hearing him recite "Howl" did just that. His passion was palpable. Or so it seemed. . . . Maybe he was just trying to impress me. When I glanced over, he snarled from the side of his mouth, " 'Ginsberg was a bottom, too.' *Hug-hug-hug.*"

After that I passed out. I may have been behind the gun store for twenty minutes, or an entire day. When I came to, he was fully dressed and clutching a shotgun.

"You know I have to kill you," he said.

It was hard to tell if he was serious. You think Cheney, you don't think joke. But the shotgun in his hand was not smiling. "Remember Harry?"

"Harry Whittington? The guy you accidentally shot in the face? When you were quail hunting?"

By way of response, he thrust the muzzle toward my face and yelped, "BLAMMO!" It was the first time I saw him smile. And I quickly wished he'd stop. That rictus grin was scarier than his persistent scowl.

"Quail's a front," he said, looming over me. "Only *quail* I ever wanted to shoot was spelled with a *y*. Lightweight by the name of Dan."

Here, finally, was the proverbial Dark Force of legend. He raised his shotgun and racked it. "There was no hunting accident," he went on, talking out of the side of his mouth. "I heard Harry was two-timing me. That bastard."

"You mean it was a lovers' spat?"

"I shot him in the face." He sneered his trademark sneer. "But I was aiming for his huevos."

That double barrel was still pointed my way. But my lover seemed to have withdrawn into himself. Indeed, to my amazement, he wiped away a tear. This was my chance.

I began to back away. One step. Two . . . Three. I felt behind me for the door. My fingers grazed the knob. Got it! But just as I prepared to make my escape, Dick Cheney lowered the gun, turned away, and, as if pulled by invisible heartstrings, moved to a closed door. Sighing audibly, he opened it. A closet. Over his shoulder, I could see within, where a single flannel shirt hung on a hanger. "Harry . . . Harry . . . Harry," he said, burying his face in the buckshot-riddled flannel.

I knew I should leave, but I was touched. We'd shared something, after all. Tenderly, Li'l Dickens rubbed the holey material on his face. Tenderly, he inhaled the must of lost desire. Here it was.

Brokeback Neo-Con. I felt myself tearing up, though at the same time I was concerned about the nagging chafe on my scrotum.

For another beat, I lingered. And then, I left him. The vice president the rest of the nation would never see. The burly, pink-thighed, sneering buffalo of love. I'll never forget you, Dick. Though, God knows, I've been trying.

MUSIC FROM EARTH

MICHELLE TEA

The night before Aidan shipped out to some other even worse part of Florida, we all went to the karaoke place on Route 12. I was wearing a bizarre outfit I'd scavenged from my mother's storm-smashed bedroom—a half-shirt with a flamingo on it and a pair of shorts so short a bit of my ass rolled out from behind a curtain of stringy, cut-off fringe. It was a scandalous look and not my style, but fuck it. My own clothing was floating in the flooded guest room, and it was so hot even at night, no power anywhere for air-conditioning, only weak fans with blades that buzzed like flies. Being half-naked felt oddly good, normal even. The wet air sat on my skin heavy as a flannel shirt. Which was what the boys stubbornly wore—Aidan and his friend Hank and his other friend

Marcus. No matter how mean the sun or how strangling the humidity, they kept themselves in their damp plaids. Aidan's little sister Angela was with us, too. She couldn't stay home because their mom wouldn't stop lobbying for Angela to have an abortion and it was oppressing her. What was worse—Angela sitting home with their Ma or coming to karaoke with Hank and Marcus, one of whom was to blame for the whole thing? Their drama was like a TV left on in the background, a soap opera you're watching with half an eye while doing something else. I felt exhausted from cleaning felled debris, a steady diet of canned tuna, and not enough water. The karaoke outing would have been awesome, a relief, if it weren't so shadowed by the occasion it was marking—Aidan's last night free before he shipped out and into the army.

The karaoke parlor had been on the news show me and Ma watched once the generator was running. The parlor was the only business left standing on a stretch of road that had held a tackle shop and a sandwich shop and a hairdresser. Everything was gone but the karaoke place, and the man who owned it, crazed with gratitude, was offering free karaoke to everyone. Aidan took his truck, me and Angela squished beside him in the tight cab. Angela's belly wasn't terribly pregnant yet; it just looked like the belly of a teenaged alcoholic, a swell above the waist of her jeans. Hank and Marcus were spread out in the truck bed next to their dogs with their ropey leashes. Hank and Marcus leaned up on their elbows, clutching beers, pointing and hollering at the catastrophe we blew by. *Ohw! Ohw!* Their cries sounded wet and far away behind the glass, clipped by the speed of the truck. They hollered at the trees at the edge of the road, whole trees knocked from the ground, their roots splayed, stiff tendrils grasping at the air.

Giant palm leaves and strips of bark lay soggy on the pavement. I thought about a wind so harsh it flayed trees, a razor gust. The tall metal signs advertising hamburgers and gas for miles looked like they'd been mauled by monster trucks. Slabs of metal hung peeled from posts. The front of a jewelry store was just gone. That store had been on the news, too, footage of the squat bald owner picking through the rubble for jewels while a cluster of cops stood near, making sure he wasn't set upon by looters. Aidan's head-lights lit up shattered glass as we passed, then left it in darkness. He drove slow because all the streetlights were out and many were downed, wet logs bumping up against the felled trees, the whole mess tangled with loops of rubbery wire and wet leaves.

Holy goddamn, Angela said, her snout pressed up against the glass, her eyes picking out shapes in the dark. *There's a boat,* she narrated. *There's a couch, there's fridge or something—a stove?* Her hands with their chipped and bitten nails were folded under her belly, cradling the thought of it. *How long you think it'll take to get normal here? Not that it was ever normal, but you know.* She gave me a look, like we were in on knowing that this place wasn't normal, the two of us together in a vehicle of boys who thought this road was the whole world, more or less. Behind us Hank and Marcus tossed their empties to shatter into the street, and the dogs howled.

The karaoke place was not a bar like the ones back in San Francisco, the gay one in the Castro where giant men sang "The Rose" or the one in the Tenderloin where hipsters crooned coun-try songs and Pat Benatar. It was a small house on the side of the road, sitting squat in a hazy halo of its own light. The only work-ing streetlamp in miles shone down on a patch of parking lot, and still more light brightened the front porch. An illuminated sign stuck with plastic letters beamed STILL OPEN SING YOUR BLUES AWAY FREE FOR HURRICANE VICTIMS. *Fuck yeah!* Angela squealed. She popped the door open and swung out from the truck before Aidan killed the engine. Her hand whumped the hood. *You should join the army more often,* she chirped. *We never do anything this fun around here!*

Hank and Marcus's wallet chains clanked on the truck as they clambered off, the dogs' collars jangling as they tied their rope leashes down. Surrounding the small house I could spot the foundations of the businesses the hurricane had lifted away. Chunky cement piles and the jagged peaks of split beams. The karaoke hut sat pristine in the middle of it all, as if it had blown over from another town, was dropped on the side of Route 12 like Dorothy's house onto a witch. Only a bit of blue tarp caught the light and revealed that it had been in the storm at all. *It's Like The Witch's House In Hansel And Gretel,* I told Aidan. *Just Sitting Here In The Middle Of Nowhere.*

It's not nowhere, it's Route 12, Aidan said. *Route 12's always been here and this karaoke place has always been on Route 12, and just because you've never been to either place don't mean it didn't exist before you showed up.* Aidan banged out the car and joined his people on the front porch, walking in long, shit-kicking strides. His baseball hat was shoved brim-first into his back pocket; Hank and Marcus both wore theirs. I sat in the cab and watched them smoking and smacking at each other, the tongues of their work boots sticking up over the cuffs of their jeans, holes in the flannels tossed over their T-shirts. I knew a dozen queer girls back home who tried to look like them, and Hank and Marcus would at the very least joke about kicking their ass. This was the last time I'd ever have to hang out with any of them. Perhaps Angela would wander through the backyard to smoke cigarettes and talk, but I wouldn't be able to keep smoking with her, not with her baby getting bigger there inside her stomach. Hank and Marcus were Aidan's friends, not mine. Possibly Aidan wasn't even my friend. Just someone I got stuck with while at my mom's in Florida, because what else do you do while at your mom's in Florida except forget you're gay and fuck a hick?

Off to the side, Angela stood looking out into the darkness, blowing Marlboro smoke up through the grid of her bangs hung long over her mouth. Aidan thought I was being a snob, and I figured I should just accept it—that I was a snob, that I would never see this place as the real world, a reasonable place to live, but as a sub-terrain of disaster and stunted options and kitsch. The armored muscle of an alligator, and the seashell sculpture of that same alligator leaning against a seashell palm and smoking a seashell cigar. The upturned corpse of an alligator in the middle of the road, it's scaled belly torn open and looted by vultures. I would only ever see Aidan as some weird *other,* first as a boy in a Dunkin' Donuts uniform dropping stale turds of Munchkins into a box; soon as a boy in a sandy camouflage, tearing away his own self in order to merge with something larger, the way a storm wrenches a roof from its house. And into the hole will come rain and mud and destruction.

The dude who ran the karaoke place seemed mad with near-death and generator fumes. The cluster of gas-chugging machines sputtered and hummed behind the building, keeping the place aglow and powering the machines playing synthesized approximations of the hits of the ages. I could hear the electronic tinkle of "Blue Velvet" faint behind the generators' roar. As promised on the news, the karaoke rooms were free; coolers of melted ice bobbed with free plastic bottles of water.

We're drinking beer tonight, 'cause my brother is joining the service tomorrow, Angela told the proprietor, whose face wrinkled and shook at her words.

No alcohol, I'm sorry, drink the water, please, as much as you want, he moved his arms at us in a weird hula, like he was pushing waves of clean water toward us. He was a Japanese man whose hair gleamed with a grimy coat of grease—sweat from the heat and sweat from panic. I wonder what situation had brought him to this random place in Florida, and if his life was better for being here.

Our boy's going in the army, Hank said, clapping his paw heavy on Aidan's back. *Tonight's his last night, man, you gotta let us celebrate. This could be his last week alive, bro!*

Marcus snorted into his sleeve and Aidan shook the hand from his back, murmuring, *Dude!* Angela spun and whacked Hank, the bottom of her beer bottle almost clipping his jaw. *Why would you say that, you sick fucker? Don't you ever say that, take that back!*

No, no! the proprietor waved his hands in front of us, breaking up the energy. *We're all alive here! We're all celebrating! Do what you like, that's okay. Take some water for later. You all have houses?*

Yes, sir, Angela said. She held her beer bottle behind her back, demurely, and bowed a bit. Hank touched his jaw.

kills an enemy, someone in the audience dies, one of the mothers, or fathers, or one of the replica fighters. And the audience, except for the fighter, is weeping the entire time, and they reach up toward the screen. No, please, no, you are killing us, you are killing yourself. But the fighter cannot hear the voices; the fighter does not see the film.

I joined the rest of the platoon. They were all fairly well drunk and had each already gone upstairs with a girl, so they were happy, too. And they seemed not too pissed off about the pogues. There was Aerosmith or some crap coming through the amps, and they could barely hear me, so I signaled them into the corridor. I told them about Cash, and Professor puked, I don't know if because he was so fucked up or from the idea of being ass-raped. We double-timed up to Cash's room.

PFC BROCKNER

I used the ether on Taro, and he was angry and hurt for a few days, and he threatened to kick me out of his life, but I told him I'd tell all to his parents, and he calmed down. And that's how I fucked him from then on, with help from the ether. I missed the noise, the noise of fucking is sometimes the best part, me in the man's ass and him jerking off at the same time, coming at the same time. But I made my own noise and still we gave each other head without the ether, and head is of course always pleasant.

I knew that I would never stop using the ether. Ether equaled power. As a marine, power surrounded me. The power of rank, of weapons, of machinery. The power of violence. One fist of iron, one fist of steel, they told us in boot camp, mean green killing machine: born to fight, trained to kill, ready to die, but never will.

But I had no power. I'd lost rank in the States after I fucked up an overhaul on a five-ton engine, and I barely qualified with the rifle and pistol, and I had nearly drowned in the pool. I changed air filters and windshield wipers and kept the logbooks. The ether would be my power. Let them have their guns.

When Operation Desert Shield started, I knew my unit would be deployed. We were part of the Expeditionary Unit for the 3rd Marine Division. We were en route on the tenth of August and staged at the port at Jabal Munifah on the twelfth, a classic clusterfuck, jarheads living in tents that Division had acquired from the Bedouins. Inside a tent where you'd expect a harem and ancient Mideast sex action, with grapes and palm fronds, instead you'd find jarheads swatting flies and drinking Evian or San Pellegrino.

And the enemy over 150 clicks away, raping and killing in Kuwait, but still we were assigned guard duty with weapons locked and loaded, so every few days some idiot would be cleaning his weapon, forget to unload, and shoot himself in the thigh or nail his buddy in the back of the head.

My platoon guarded the Port Authority tower, and this worked well for me. The tower had air-conditioning pumping through it all day, and the lounge area was equipped with a fully stocked wet bar. The two guys running the port were Brits. They didn't mind us hitting the bar after duty. So of course we would. Drinking Cape Cods and Absolut martinis up was a pleasure we hadn't expected. The bathrooms were fixtured in gold, and the showers, outfitted with three or four spigots and a bench, could've fit ten people easy. It was a queer bathhouse waiting to happen right in the middle of the desert.

I started sleeping with one of the Brits, Simon. He had bad teeth and he drank way too much scotch. I don't see how a single boat made it through the port during his watch. He spent much of his time quoting Samuel Johnson and T. S. Elliot, swaying with a bottomless tumbler in one hand and the microphone in the other, pausing between directions to ships to wink at me or smile his brown, broken-up teeth. But we were great lovers. He insisted that he wasn't queer or even bi. He opposed screwing whores, and the Saudi women were untouchable. He'd screwed the wives of a few of his co-workers, but those situations never ended well. I would call him a straight fag as I entered him from behind.

My sergeant noticed I spent my off-duty hours in the tower, and he asked questions about my friend Simon, so I implemented evasive action. Word had it that a navy captain sold blow jobs for five bucks apiece. I tracked her down and covered her for my guard team, all twelve of us plus the sergeant. I brought her up to the lounge at the tower and she sucked us off, Simon and his co-worker Thomas as well. After everyone dispersed she asked for a drink, so I made her a Cosmopolitan. After three or four Cosmos, she started touching my knee and laughing with her neck quirked sideways, her pretty, long fingers wrapped around the sweaty stem of her drink. She wanted to seduce me, and she told me so. I lied and said I had a wife back home, a wife who didn't mind me getting blow jobs but nothing more. She wouldn't stop with her sexy routine, and told me not to worry, that it wouldn't cost anything, and soon she had her uniform off except her panties. She said, If you're not going to fuck me, at least watch me masturbate.

She arched way back and pulled her hand out of her panties when she came, and there were beads of sweat on her forehead and nose. She reminded me of Egon Schiele's *Reclining Woman with Legs Apart*, her body contorted in libidinous repose.

SERGEANT SAVINE

Esmeralda petted Cash's head as we entered the room. He said over and over, I'll kill the motherfucker. Professor went into the bathroom and puked again while Mathis, Boner, and Preacher Boy looked at Cash with flat amazed faces. Preacher Boy ran down to the basement to look for a corpsman, and we left Esmeralda with Cash. We had to find the Ether Bandit. Bad shit would soon be going down, and we were going to be the arbiters of the bad shit and the world should stand the fuck by.

PFC BROCKNER

Simon started getting uppity, uppity little whore, I called him. He swung at me one night when I wouldn't stop. He said, Please stop. You have to be fucking stupid to use the words *Please stop,* so I kept fucking, and harder, and I am a big man, so it was not hard to continue. He swung again and hit me in the jaw, which I barely felt, and I beat him severely, but not his ugly face. I pummeled his kidneys and chest and the back of his head until he cried and my knuckles and fingers were swollen and stuck in a fist, and he continued to cry and I left him there in the lounge, moaning like a little bitch.

The first time I used the ether in the desert was at a USO show out in the mining areas near Ash Shama. It was an amusing show, Brooke Shields singing and playing off the Muslim-censored jokes of Steve Martin and Bob Hope. Amusing but not funny. Hope told a joke about going blind from masturbation, and that's the only one I remember. Marines were dropping from heat exhaustion, some of the units having hiked fifteen or more miles for the morale boost, guys trying to stand on tip-toes and locking their knees, and that's when they'd drop. The corpsmen had a heat exhaustion tent set up, thirty cots with IV drips, and half a dozen exam rooms. I always carried my jar of ether and a skivvy shirt in my ass-pack, and I hadn't planned it, but in all the mess of bodies and the sweaty movement of troops out of the area after the show, I slipped into the medical tent and one of the exam rooms where a young marine lay dizzy and confused on a cot, maybe hallucinating. I rubbed his shoulder and told him he'd be okay, in a few hours he'd be up and around, and I covered his pretty face with the ether rag and he was out quickly. I could hear from the other side of the curtain corpsmen and doctors shouting orders and marines on cots moaning and bitching. I turned him on his side, still hooked up to his IV, and pulled myself out. I pulled his trousers down past his knees. I spit on the end of my dick and started slowly in. I wanted to spank him, I wanted to make noise, but I couldn't. I entered him slowly and the blood began and that helped with getting in and then I was in all the way. When I finished I wiped myself off with the ether shirt and I left the young, pretty marine's trousers down at his knees and a bloody mess covering his ass and the olive drab cot. I kissed his hip. Let them have their guns.

SERGEANT SAVINE

We assumed the Ether Bandit had left the building. But we broke up into teams and searched every room on every floor, looking for a clue. I went down to the basement. The pogues and line grunts had broken up their party, and Thomas and his girls cleaned the mess of broken bottles and cigarette butts and used condoms. It struck me as funny how no matter where we were in the world, the Marine Corps handed out condoms. Always cheap condoms, Shank usually, or sometimes Splendor, but they handed them out even in the middle of the desert, which meant to me they knew the whorehouse existed. Thomas had to be kicking down to someone, either whores or money or both. Probably he was dealing drugs as well, but he never brought us in on that. He must've figured not to with the snipers, we were all hard motherfuckers, hard, crazy motherfuckers with the cinema of war going on in our eyes, and he must've known we wouldn't touch his shit. In Vietnam the fighters were all fucked up on dope, and they did very little good for the battle plan. Sure, it's glamorous, shooting smack or smoking stick before going into the shit, it's all glamour in those bullshit movies, but let me see a sniper put a bullet in an enemy officer's skull from a grand out while he's high as fuck on any kind of dope. Won't fucking happen. Sure, before we joined The Suck we all daydreamed of getting high in the bush and taking out an entire enemy patrol, but the fighter doesn't need movies. The civilian and the pogue need movies.

Professor screamed, I found something, I found a skivvy shirt! He ran down the third-floor corridor with an olive drab skivvy shirt balled up in his right fist. He shoved it in my face, and I smelled the faint sweet scent of ether, and also the muddy stench of blood and shit and come. We had the same thought at the same time—look in the neckband for a name neatly stamped in black, half-inch block letters. BROCKNER BF. No one we knew. A pogue of course, a fucking pogue running around ass-raping for fun.

Esmeralda went home to her husband. A corpsman stitched Cash up and gave him some pills for the pain. Nothing could be done for the mind fucking he'd received, worse than a boot camp mind fuck, worse than all of the fuck fuck games ever thrown his way. A damn good thing it happened at Thomas's. With medical supplies and a corpsman nearby, the word wouldn't spread. And with the word not getting out, we could complete our reconnaissance.

PFC BROCKNER

I started taking chances. After the USO show seeming so easy, and so nice to be in that young marine's ass, I couldn't help myself.

Very early one morning, I raped a jarhead at the port. I couldn't sleep and went down to the head for a shit-shower-shave. I wore flip-flops and shorts and nothing else, with my war belt over my shoulders and my shower gear in my ass-pack. The Saudi mornings were pleasant, ripe cool floating in from the coast, taste of salt and sky before the blistering heat came down to blur the world. The heads at the port weren't plush like in the tower, but they were kept clean. I heard water running when I walked in, and whistling coming over the shower wall. A young marine, I imagined, who finally got a call patched through to his girlfriend, the girlfriend he needed assurance from that she hadn't fucked his best friend or brother. He whistled away, I don't know what tune, but he sounded happy. I stripped down and walked into the steamy shower, and we gave the obligatory hello nod that straight men give each other in public showers. Yes I am naked and so are you and maybe we will take quick appraising glances, but that's all.

He kept whistling, which at first bothered me. Then I admired the boldness of it—I am so happy over my girlfriend I will whistle in this shower at 3:00 A.M. in Saudi Arabia, here I am gearing up for war, but I will whistle even with this stranger near me in the shower. I took more than appraising glances and started getting hard—blue veins—his solid fine ass, the thin, fine flow of water snaking down his back and onto his ass, down his muscular legs, across the back of his knees, down his Achilles' tendon and slithering onto the concrete deck, into the drain.

I dried off and set up for a shave and prepared the ether shirt. He continued to whistle as he exited the shower and worked his way toward a sink behind me. My face lathered, I looked at him and asked him his unit. He mumbled off an air wing squadron, something about electronics. I told him I was a grunt with the 3rd Marines. Once he lathered his face, hot water steaming from the sink and obscuring the mirror, I covered his mouth and nose with the ether shirt. He fought. He caught me in the ribs with an elbow and he pulled on my right ear, yanking so hard I thought he'd rip it off, but I held the shirt close and hard to his face, and he went under. Too much ether could cause death, not enough would give the person a good buzz—a good buzz they could easily snap out of. I dragged him into the shower. I had trouble opening him up, and I came quickly, just barely inside. I pointed a cold shower at him and cleaned myself, washing the shaving cream from my face, washing my crotch, his blood and the foamy shaving cream mixing together and trickling off of me and down into the drain.

SERGEANT SAVINE

A few weeks after Cash's rape, Johnson, at Division ConAd, tracked Brockner down for us. He was a pogue, 6th CSSB, a god-damn mechanic.

PFC BROCKNER

And then I really fucked up. I went out to the whorehouse that Simon's friend Thomas ran, thinking it would be good cover. I'd drink some drinks and listen to music and party, probably not even take a whore upstairs, just buy her a few drinks and let her sit on my lap for a dance or two. But the same old whorehouse scene bored me, just like in Oki or the PI, so I walked around the hospital thinking I might be able to break into a med locker and find some painkillers that I could sell or trade for guard shifts. On the fourth floor I heard a whore screaming and hollering and a jarhead fucking her rough. I leaned against the wall opposite their room and watched through the open door. The jarhead fucked her from behind, and he had a pretty body and so did she. She had long dark Flip hair that was flying all over the place, stuck in his mouth and hers too, the both of them sweating, the both of them soaking wet with sweat and sex. After he came, she got up quickly, scurrying around the floor for her clothes. He was angry, asking why she always leaves so soon, why she goes back to the basement to fuck other jarheads, why doesn't she stay the night? She cussed at him in a mixture of English and Tagalog, telling him he was just a boy and that she had a life to live, that she had children and a husband in the Philippines she had to support, and what the fuck did he have to do every day but wake up and shit? He didn't respond, and really, what could he have said? She rushed out of the room as I backed into the opposite doorway. I heard another jarhead coming up the stairwell with a woman, and they entered a room at the other end of the hall.

My jarhead was on the bed, belly down, crying, wadding up the corner of the pillow with his fist. He screamed *whore* and *fuck*. I covered his face with the ether shirt and he fought, but not much, not like the guy at the port.

And here is how I fucked myself: I rushed out of the room, knowing that any minute another jarhead would be heading up with a girl, and I didn't close my ass-pack. As I ran down the hall or a stairwell, my ether shirt fell out, my ether shirt with my name stamped in the neckline, just like they teach at boot camp, centered above the tag. I didn't notice this until I made it back to the port. And then I had only to wait.

SERGEANT SAVINE

We decided to make it real simple. We'd abduct him and take him out to the middle of the desert and make up a little hell for him, let Cash work on him, work the kind of evil we'd been trained to practice on the enemy, but so little going on with the enemy, still not the real shit going down, just minor missions across the border, so why not let this pogue rapist catch a bit of our fury?

We hung around the tower at the port where Brockner performed guard duty and watched him for a few days. He rarely left. His platoon members brought him hot chow. He only exited the tower for morning and afternoon company formation.

One afternoon when one of his platoon mates headed in with a plate of hot chow, Cash gave the guy a note for Brockner. We found out from ConAd Johnson that Brockner grew up in Winnemuca, Nevada, and he'd joined the corps on the Buddy Program with a Corporal Jennings. We forged a note from Jennings:

Hey, fucker, I'm here now, too. Far ways from Winnemuca. Come down and let's shoot the shit.

It was a chance, because maybe he still knew Jennings, maybe they'd butt-fucked in high school or they kept in touch, and he knew Jennings was on nuclear duty in Juneau, Alaska. But we had to try. Plus, all the guys we knew who joined on the Buddy Program hated their buddy and blamed their buddy for royally fucking them and had lost touch with their buddy. But if the buddy shows up in your area, you can't just say fuck you.

Brockner walked out ten minutes later. Cash head-butted him, knocked him out cold. We threw him in the back of the Hummer, tied and gagged him, and diddy'd out to the middle of the desert, out to the long-distance range, ready for a little show-and-tell, some live fire.

PFC BROCKNER

Of course Jennings wasn't in the desert. But the writing on the note looked like his. I walked out the door and the guy took me down. I came to in the back of a Hummer, facedown, hands and feet tied, mouth gagged. I was burning up, the drive train spinning below me, the bed of the Hummer at least 150 degrees. I knew who they were. Thomas told Simon that the Ether Bandit had hit a sniper at his whorehouse and that the snipers were pissed off and ready to take someone out.

SERGEANT SAVINE

I'd acquired ether from the Regimental Med locker. I figured a bit of his own, a bit of his own back in him. Cash wanted to beat him, to beat him silly and dumb and knock out all of his teeth, to fuck him with a flashlight and leave him for dead in the desert.

Cash dragged him out of the Hummer by his feet. The afternoon burned straight down into the desert, burned the desert flat, the heat radiating off the sand and swirling in your lungs and covering your body, blanketing your body with fire and an intimate feeling of death.

Cash kicked him in the face so hard the pressure bandage I'd used to gag him went from white to red in seconds. Cash said to him, I bled out of my ass like that, and he kicked him again. I reached down and pulled the bandage out of his mouth so he wouldn't choke on his blood. Cash repeatedly punched him in the face but the Ether Bandit made no noise, his face bloody and his nose badly broken. He spit out three teeth. Cash said, Fag-rape me and you die ugly. Cash kicked him in the ribs and the face, and he still made no noise. He was strong, and I figured he could take this all day, all night. I kicked him in the head. I pulled the ether out, daubed it on his skivvy shirt that we'd found at the whorehouse, and covered his bloody face.

PFC BROCKNER

I remembered his pretty face. The other one covered my mouth and nose with my ether shirt and I thought, Okay then, let's do it, nothing I haven't had before. He didn't keep it on long enough, or use enough, so it felt like a good buzz, like coming down from a weekend of good clean drugs and dancing until 6:00 A.M. They ripped my trousers down and turned me over. I could make out their voices, and which voice belonged to whom. The guy I raped hit me over the head with something hard, and then said, This flashlight is bigger than your dick. How are you gonna like it up inside you?

The flashlight split me open—the tearing of flesh and muscle and, as the metal went deeper, the ripping of my intestines—and I felt the metal in my stomach, buried that deep inside. I told him to fuck harder, to get deeper inside of me, that I wanted to feel it in my throat. This pissed him off, the guy I raped, and the other guy said, He's fucking crazy. I knew they wanted to hear me cry, they wanted to hear me beg them to stop, to whimper like a bitch, but I would not give them that, I wouldn't give them anything they wanted.

SERGEANT SAVINE

The Ether Bandit was as hard and crazy as a fighter. He was half conscious, and he told Cash to fuck him harder. And Cash did but it didn't matter. There wasn't shit we could do to make him pay, there wasn't shit we could do besides put a bullet in him, because we weren't going to flashlight-fuck him to death.

I pulled Cash away from him. I removed the flashlight. The Ether Bandit's ass was a mess, blood and muscle and tissue exploding from his insides out. I applied a pressure bandage to his wound and injected him in the hip with two morphine syrettes.

We drove to our battalion bivouac near Rish Qahwah. Cash wasn't satisfied, but I told him he had to be, that what we'd done was enough to kill a man, and the Ether Bandit hadn't backed down, so we had no choice but to let him live.

PFC BROCKNER

Late that night a platoon from the 5th Marines found me as they drove through the desert on their way to a night fire. The grunts medevac'd me to the infirmary of the U.S.S. *Peleliu*. My name appeared on the Division crime blotter as another victim of the Ether Bandit. A Naval Investigative Service officer interviewed me, and I gave a perfect physical description of myself, but he didn't notice me because he was so close and afraid for his own ass.

By the time I recovered, the war had been over for a few weeks.

VICTORY GARDEN

JAMI ATTENBERG

We met in the bushes, she and I. That's where everyone goes nowadays to get their fun on around here, ever since we had to give up the cars. We gave up the cars without a fight, because there wasn't much oil left to put in them. The president decided to start a bunch of wars (Q: How many wars can you start at once? A: Four.) and he asked us to donate our cars so we could build weapons, and we all said, sure, wasn't like we were using them anyway. And just like that it became illegal to have a car. They throw people in jails now. They will fuck you up if you have a car. Now we walk everywhere or ride our bikes (the bikes weren't worth their time), and when we want to make out in the backseats of cars we just use the bushes instead.

I wasn't making out that night. My girl had left me to get married to a soldier who was going off to war. (The one in India, I think.) "No offense," she said. "Benefits." She had met him at one of the barn social nights. Slow dances under rotting beams, punch spiked with government-issued vodka, an enormous American flag pinned to the wall. Girls are recruited starting junior year. There are posters in the cafeteria. An open invitation to the young ladies.

Say goodbye before they're gone.

I had heard stories, also, of what happened outside the barn, in the back, near the pile of old tractor tires, under a thrush of trees. A soldier asks a young lady to take a walk, and she says yes—she has to, this might be their only chance to meet, to connect, to fall in love—and he puts his hand on the back of her neck and squeezes it when they walk out the door together.

But it has nothing to do with a walk; it's all about fucking. There are lines of our local girls bent over the tractor tires, their skirts pushed up just high enough on their backs so that their asses are swinging in the air, moving back and forth while the soldiers stick their pricks in them. Some of the girls are on their knees, too, and they suck and lick under and around and all over, a fury of motion with their mouths; these girls are serving their country and then suddenly their faces are damp, wet with the soldier's come, or it runs down the back of their throat, or if he is a gentleman he misses her entirely and hits the tractor tire instead, the white fluid glistening against the rubber in the moonlight.

God bless America. That's what they grunt under their breaths.

I did not know my girlfriend had been attending the barn socials. It only took her a few months before she found the man for her. It had made me crazy, not just the thought of her leaving me but that she had snuck around on me for so long. Was I really dumb or was she really smart? For a while, I could not wrap my head around who she was, or how I was supposed to let her go.

Still, marrying a soldier was your best bet for a good life. They say there's only three ways out of any town these days: join the army, marry the army, or start walking. (I can't join myself. One leg is shorter than the other, so I walk a little bit funny. It's not enough so you would notice, only enough that I can't be asked to fight, to serve, to protect, to destroy.) So I could not hold it against her. We had just graduated from high school. I did not put up a fight. I had nothing to give her but a ride on the back of my bicycle.

Although it is a smooth ride.

I was alone, taking the dog for one of the nightly long walks that had replaced the time I spent with my girlfriend. We were alone together, the dog and I, but I think we both wanted to be near people even if we couldn't be with them. The dog always pulled me that direction, down by the park, and he sniffed and howled a little bit. We were lured by the bushes, the sounds and the smells of all the kids from school, the kisses and the moans. I could picture the bright purple marks forming on their necks. Everyone was so happy and free. The air smelled fresh and green and sexy. We were young.

This is what they do now. They start at one end of town at sunset, and one by one, the kids show up and make the march to the park. By night, the streets are full of kids walking and talking, sharing whatever news they heard their parents whispering about that day. Sometimes they scrawl things on walls with chalk. Names of enemies, dates of drafts, lists of the missing and the found. A good piece of dirt can get you laid before dusk breaks. (Not that they're in any hurry: Curfews disappeared with the cars. How far could anyone get? What kind of trouble could they find on their feet?) And then there they are, at last, at the park, in the dark. Kids fall in love in the bushes, babies are made, mosquitoes bite. Where you're born is where you'll live is where you'll die.

Sometimes I miss oil.

They gather near a patch of American elms; that's where it shifts. Maybe they're thinking about how they're doing their part for our country, our great nation. They swig alcohol from paper bags, move their weight from foot to foot, dance to the sound of the cicadas chirping from the leaves. I've done that dance before. And then they pair off eventually, wander away from the elms, closer to the bushes, pointing at a constellation or lying down and hoping for shooting stars. A shooting star guarantees that first kiss. After the first kiss—maybe they roll around on the ground for a bit—it's a just short walk to the bushes that spiral up every year higher to the sky, farther away from the earthly pleasures beneath them.

They've been calling it "the rustle" lately.

Not everyone hangs out in the bushes. Some kids like to pair up on a Friday and pick the dirt weed on the back roads. That stuff was never strong enough to smoke until a few years ago; there was a shift in the air after the explosion in Council Bluffs, and now what looks harmless can send you flying for two days straight. Those are the kids who don't care at all about going anywhere, although every so often one of them will pack up a bag of weed and head on down the highway. They never come back.

And then there's me. I like to walk, and watch everyone. We were tracing a little path when I met her, me and the dog. She was coming up toward us, a huddle in the darkness of sweaters, a sturdy coat, and a gigantic backpack. She balanced each step with a walking stick. We stopped as we approached, and stood in front of each other, and then a girl let out a loud and very final-sounding moan from the bushes, and the leaves rustled.

"Hi," she said. "I'm lost." She didn't look scared at all, though maybe she should have been, wandering around in the middle of nowhere, near all those squirming bodies in the bushes.

"Where are you trying to go?" I said, though I had a pretty good idea.

"I heard there was a place for people like me around here," she said. She shifted her backpack up on her back and lifted her head up, and the moon and the stars hit her face and I could see that her skin was clear and her eyes were dark and focused and determined, and then she smiled, not warily but aware. There was a sliver of space between her two front teeth. I wanted to insert my tongue between the space and let it lie there for a while and see what it felt like. The dog liked her, too. He sniffed at her feet and then rested at them.

She was making her way to Los Angeles, she told me. We'd seen a few of her kind passing through before. Los Angeles had seceded from the union a while back, when the first rumblings of the car reclamation had started. They had fought the hardest of anywhere. They loved their cars the most. Foreign investors in the film industry had kept them stocked with oil, and our government allowed them certain freedoms as long as they kept churning out movies. We had all heard stories of a city trapped in gridlock, but people were migrating there from all over the country. To a place that *moved*.

It was a real shame about Detroit, what happened there.

"You're a ways away from the shelter," I told her, but I said I'd walk her in the right direction. It was a nice night. From the bushes we heard two voices jumble together in laughter, and then a man said, "I love you." I offered to carry her bag for her, and she judged it, judged me, and then handed it over.

As we walked she told me about life back east. Her husky voice perfectly matched the sound of the crunch of gravel under our feet. She was from Philadelphia, and like every other city out there, there weren't too many trees left, let alone bushes. There were lines every night at the few parks that remained open to the public (the military had built up housing units wherever there was room), and the government charged admission. A fee to flirt. If you couldn't afford that, it was all alleyways for you.

She said she got sick of the feel of cold cement against her ass.

I closed my eyes for a second and I was there with her in the dark, near a darkened building, maybe a courthouse or a library or a shopping center. She was pressed up against the wall, and the brick crumbled behind her when I touched it with my fingertips. I rubbed the dust off on her neck and chest, and then I moved my hand down to her breast and throttled her nipple. I squeezed so hard. I wanted her to feel good. And then I put my hand between her legs and it was warm down there, and I knew she was going to smell sweet and taste sweet, and I pulled my hand up and put a finger in my mouth, and it tasted delicious. My prick rumbled against my pants, and I stopped thinking about it.

She told me she was scared of the things we had to give up. There were other things besides the cars; we all could see it coming. Babies, for one, and that had already happened; it was law now, in almost every state. Every teenage girl goes on the pill as soon as she gets her period. Pills they could make easy; it's the condoms that were hard to manufacture without the oil. And we were running out of room, any fool could tell you that. Not so much here in the heartland but all around the edges of the country, and in practically any big city, people were jammed into homes like cars on a freeway during rush hour. At least the way I imagined that would look. I hadn't seen too many rush hours in my life.

I will admit I acted up when I went into the draft office my senior year of high school. That was during the war with China, and there was just no way I was going. I exaggerated my walk, the gap in height between one leg and the other. I wanted to make sure the recruiter knew. I'm sure I would have disappointed my father, only he was already dead. Long gone, eight years. And not enough of him had been left behind to roll over in his grave.

I did not tell her this story as we walked. I thought she would like me less if she knew. I let her talk instead. "I know I shouldn't complain," she said. "I know how lucky I am, how lucky we all are. We live in the safest place in the world." It was true: we won every war we started.

"But I just wanted to see what it was like," she said. She threw her arms up toward the sky and all around. "Out there." She stopped and touched me, turned me toward her. "Not that I care about the cars so much. Although I guess I do care. I just wanted to be somewhere new."

And then because I wanted to impress her, because she had impressed me with her ache and desire and energy, even though I didn't know her at all, even though she could have been lying about who she was and why she was there, even though I might never see her again, even though she was tired and dirty and she smelled of the earth (or maybe because of it), even though I could have been trading in my freedom—because who was she after all? Only a girl I had met on a dirt road—I said to her, "Do you want to see something really cool?"

We shifted direction toward my home. She dug the trail behind us with the stick, like we were headed for a witch in the woods somewhere. We made it home quickly; we were both excited. She dropped her bag on the front porch. I took the dog off the leash and let him run around in circles in the backyard. We walked toward the small island of trees and bushes behind my house. He barked, nervous, but I ignored him. I had nothing to lose. I held her hand and cleared us a path through the bushes, until we came upon it.

A 2017 Chevy. The roof was missing, and the leather had been beaten down by the rain and snow. Everything else was rusted. But still we slid in the backseat immediately.

She started to cry, but I think maybe she was laughing, too.

"It's just a useless piece of junk," I said. "It's not that special."

"No, it's really nice," she said.

I put my arm around her and we slouched down in the seats. "There should be a radio playing," she said. "Classic rock." So I sang, my voice echoing in the trees. I sang her every song I remembered, songs that smelled of revolution, songs of the days when my father was alive, when she and I were still young and knew nothing, nothing of war or fear or what it was like to have to walk forever, and then when I was done with those, I made up a few new ones just for her.

DESERT SHIELD

LYDIA MILLET

The mission of our troops is wholly defensive . . . they will not
initiate hostilities.

> —President George Bush, press conference,
> August 9, 1990, scripted speech

I think it is beyond the defense of Saudi Arabia. So I think it's
beyond that.

> —President George Bush, press conference,
> August 9, 1990, Q&A

My Boy Scout in the White House knew where he was going from the start. He had consulted his pocket compass, and the needle was quivering between "War Powers Resolution" and "First Strike."

It was an auspicious and exciting time, what with the large-scale mobilization of our troops, by mid-September costing taxpayers about twenty-nine million dollars a day. A bargain. You can't put a price tag on glory. Everyone and his brother felt downright historic; it had the momentous panache of an impending WWIII. We were an empire again, and it was scoring 75 percent approval ratings for G.B. He had been Born Again in the opinion polls, and I was watching his ascent there somewhat fearfully. Because we were still living in hungry Reaganite country; my fellow Americans would line up behind G.B. only as long as he stalked like a predator, slavered at the chops and pretended to wipe his drooling fangs on a sleeve.

Russell had a new synthetic hipbone and had been prescribed a couple of months' worth of Percocet, so he felt he was sitting pretty. He lay on the sofa all the time in front of the TV, which forced me to use the second, smaller TV upstairs for my sessions with G.B. That was working out fine, until one night there was a realignment in our domestic geometry.

I'd stopped on my way home to buy a goodwill present for Russki in the form of twelve Original Glazed Krispy Kreme doughnuts. Russell had virtually no appetite, so I looked forward to the pleasure of consuming the lion's share myself. Imagine my shocked chagrin when, green-and-white box in hand, I entered my base of operations and saw that he had company.

Russell's complete lack of friends, or even casual acquaintances, had long been a selling point for me. His isolation from a larger community was both liberating and complimentary. To find him lying in the living room with his legs up on the sofa arm and his teeth on an end table, sharing visibly stiff whiskeys with what appeared to be an Appalachian mountain man, was unnerving to say the least.

The mountain man had a matted gray beard that hung almost to his waist. I would not have been surprised to find small animals nesting in it. He was wearing a safari jacket of Lawrence of Arabia vintage, which apparently had not been doused with water since the turn of the century. He committed his first faux pas right off the bat, in what was to prove a defining moment for me. When I came into the room, and was standing staring at them at a loss for words, he jerked a thumb in my direction and asked of Russell, "Who's the roly-poly?"

And then he proceeded to eat eight of the doughnuts himself. Little did he know, at that instant, that he had made his worst enemy.

The mountain man turned out to be an old comrade-in-arms from Russell's service days. Or post-service, to be precise. After leaving our nation's armed forces in the wake of their separate Korean experiences, they had met in the VA hospital, gotten along famously, and subsequently worked together for over a decade as soldiers-for-hire, that is to say, mercenaries. It was a part of Russell's life that, until then, he hadn't shared with me, and I found it hard to believe at first. I guess I'd had some preconceptions about mercenaries. We all have our prejudices.

Anyway, our visitor went by the unlikely name of Apache and now, in his dotage, made his living as a part-time truck driver. His eighteen-wheeler was parked down the street, illegally. I was not pleased to be informed that he visited Russell on an annual basis, and was planning to stay for a week.

Leaving them to while away their time by telling tired anec-dotes of senseless brutality, I made my way to the basement and locked the door to my private chamber. This done, I repaired to the kitchen to cook them a three-course meal while developing my strategy quietly. I had quickly determined that I would work, over the first couple of days, to enlarge Apache's trust in me by playing the part of the servile domestic female.

In those months I was walking a tightrope both at home and at work, where I had started angling for a ten-cent-an-hour pay raise if they moved me to Class III. I was cannily maneuvering to optimize my personal freedom and my opportunities, in steadfast pursuit of the founding fathers' bright dream.

Apache seemed to be opening up to me by the third night, when I barbecued steaks; he tore into his sirloin ravenously and made several grunting noises that I interpreted favorably, as I sat beside Russell and diced his portion into small pieces. But the next day, when I came in at 6:00 P.M., Russki was dozing splay-legged on the bathroom floor and there were eight empty Red Hook beer bottles beside the Louis Seize. Russell looked down on beer as a weakling's drink; I knew there was only one possible culprit. Sure enough, Apache, drunk, stoned, and wandering through the house, had picked the basement lock. I came upon him standing in front of my G.B. media crucifix, leafing through my most recent policy memo file, a homegrown joint dangling from the side of his chapped mouth.

"Lady, you're fat and you're freakin' crazy," he drawled, crassly but not unaffectionately.

"This will not stand," I said, taking a hint from G.B. and clenching my jaw. "Put that down and get out of here."

"Eat me," said Apache.

An energetic struggle ensued. I was taken off-guard by his strength and agility; the hirsute old codger had lightning reflexes and evident martial arts expertise. I soon realized I had made a grave error of judgment in engaging him in combat physically. Ten minutes after hostilities had been initiated, the sour-smelling carpet of his facial hair was flowing over my face, blinding me, suffocating me, and tickling my nostrils unpleasantly, and my wrists were pinned to the floor while Apache had his way with me.

I was not new to the game, fortunately—on the contrary, I was by that time a seasoned veteran—and was able to relax eventually, to minimize abrasion. When Apache slunk away I had only two bracelets of bruises to show for my trouble, plus an incipient kidney infection and a small cut above my left eyebrow.

What does not kill us makes us stronger, and I came out of the episode extremely Firm in my Resolve. That night at supper, a tacit social understanding seemed to arise between Apache and me. So long as I did not bring up the subject of his rude Assault with Russell, he wouldn't mention his basement discoveries. (Personally I'm not sure Russ would have minded what Apache had done to me; he wasn't the jealous type, and he wasn't what you would call "overprotective" of me. I've never had an "overprotective" boyfriend, come to think of it. You don't see gerbils guarding a warthog.) We ate Tater Tots and spaghetti in sullen silence, with Russki breaking the silence occasionally to reminisce about a boyish escapade the two of them had shared in Angola.

But Apache's behavior really rankled with me. I'd had a lot of that in Max, and I figured I'd exceeded my quota. Plus I had been trying to steer clear of entanglements that dirtied me. The episode was disrespectful of G.B.

After the meal I retired to the empty guest bedroom that contained the second TV and watched taped footage of President 41 while eating ice cream until I fell asleep. I considered approaching the authorities with reference to Apache, but dismissed the notion, deciding such action would be bound to have unpleasant repercussions ultimately. I had broken my parole the year before, by relocating to take the job at the factory. (My parole officer had found only sewage work for me, and the fumes had been sparking blackouts that reminded me of those olden days on PCP.) So red tape was one of my many enemies.

With only three days remaining in Apache's planned visit, I had almost decided to let bygones be bygones when he announced to Russell and me that he was extending his vacation.

The truth of the matter is that I could not identify Apache's Achilles' heel. Every man has a weakness, and every woman, too; and it is never wise to launch a first strike without foreknowledge of the target's vulnerability. And because of the détente that had arisen between us, I had few chances for in-depth study. No matter how many meals I cooked him, I could not win over Apache to induce him to confide in me. Like G.B., I cannot be all things to all people; some of my fellow humans lack the ability to see the greatness and the wistfulness in me. Frankly, I will not stoop to teach them.

"The anchor in our world today is freedom," G.B. had said in his 1990 State of the Union. I didn't know about that metaphor at the time. If I had been G.B., I would have found myself some new speechwriters. Correct me if I'm wrong, but I'm under the distinct impression that an anchor, like a leg shackle, is there to hold us down.

Still, the sentiment was nice, and fully worthy of G.B. When he talks about freedom—and he does, he used the word *free* twenty-one times in that State of the Union address—he means it. That was becoming clear to me in the early days of what they were then calling the Persian Gulf Crisis. The thing about freedom is that the more you have, the more the next guy doesn't. It's kind of like fresh water: as long as you're upstream, there's plenty to go around. The freer you are in the mountains, the thirstier they get near the sea.

Take Max Sec, for example. If I exercised my freedom to defend myself against bodily assault, that meant that Rump lost her freedom to express sexual preference. Either way you sliced it, someone wasn't free.

And there could be no freedom for me while Apache the mountain man was ruling our roost. The sight of his beard over the breakfast table, its greasy tendrils decorated with fragments of scrambled egg, made me nauseated for an entire day as I recalled our forced intimacy. I ceased to cook for Russell and him, and I regretted that I had not yet learned how to rig up a simple incendiary device. One would have fitted snugly beneath his truck's right front wheel.

I was between a rock and a hard place. There were only so many hours I could spend on the factory floor. I tried passing the time at local bars, but I was growing highly impatient to be back, safely ensconced and media-vigilant, in my personal war room dedicated to G.B.

As Week Three of Apache's stay began, I was set in an uncomfortable routine. I would put in an hour or so of unpaid overtime at work, making sure, when possible, that my supervisor saw me; eat a microwaved dinner in the employee lounge, which resembled nothing so much as a World War II bunker; and return to the house via Skullduggery, the nearest purveyor of liquor and entertainment, around ten, when I usually found Russell and Apache snoring in their armchairs amid empty beer and whiskey bottles, a pornographic videotape playing on the TV screen. I would then sequester myself for the rest of my waking hours in the guest bedroom with G.B.

In the midst of a tortuous budget struggle, he had courageously vetoed a minor civil rights bill that didn't meet his high standards of legislative excellence: the Civil Rights Act of 1990. Congress impudently tried to override the veto, but their override fell one vote short, 66–34, and they were feeling impotent compared to G.B. Plus, G.B. had reluctantly given the rubber stamp to a couple of "revenue increases," incurring the wrath of the fiscal-minded G.O.P. Sure, he had reneged on his tax pledge, which simplistic pundits said had gotten him elected; that didn't matter to me. It was the posturing manliness of the phrase "Read my lips" that had first interested me in G.B., not the apparent substance of the no-new-taxes message. Fiscal policy is for the small-minded, for the cheap hoarders among us who begrudge the poor a buck or two of Earned Income Credit. It has never been my interest or my specialty.

Anyway, G.B. fell into a temporary public-approval tailspin—from which he would soon recover dramatically, like the true fighter pilot he used to be—and, isolated from the peons of his party, was flailing weakly. I watched him day after day on the televised campaign trail for the upcoming congressional elections, and more than once I winced. Every sting to G.B. pierced my thin skin just as deeply. At a campaign rally for a Republican candidate in Vermont, G.B. was lambasted by said candidate right up there on the podium. Even though our generous forty-first president had deigned to sit beside him in a gesture of support, Rep. Peter Smith, a freshman congressman running for reelection, said extremely rudely, "My specific disagreements with this administration are a matter of public record."

When G.B. got up to speak he was so hurt and confused that all he could say was, "We have a sluggish economy out there nationally. That's one of the reasons I favor this deficit so much."

And then he went off on the hostage situation. Even though the U.S. ambassador in Kuwait City said that the diplomats had plenty of food, G.B. charged they were "being starved by a brutal dictator." At another campaign rally in New England, he went on to say that Iraq had "committed outrageous acts of barbarism. Brutality—I don't believe that Adolf Hitler ever participated in anything of that nature."

G.B. was committing senseless gaffes left and right; he was a raging bull in a china shop. Although I felt for him, I was also worried. G.B. was supposed to be a steely pillar of strength for me.

With Week Four of Planet Apache, the leaves were falling from the trees and my frustration reached a fever pitch. I missed my personal space; I missed the pre-Apache peace and harmony. I was nervous and antsy. So on Congressional Election Day, which brought in a poor to mediocre showing for G.B. and company, I visited a doctor—something I had not done since the lead pipe incident due to the costs involved—and complained of insomnia. My hysterical tears, and the dark rings beneath my eyes, convinced her my claim was honest, and she prescribed powerful soporifics.

At home I ground several of these into a powder in the bathroom, using dead Sarah's stoneware mortar and pestle, and packed the powder into a straw with tape on both ends. On the pretext of wishing to clear away the thirty-odd beer bottles that had accumulated around Apache's nest in front of the TV, I circulated among the debris and scouted out the scene. He was apparently drinking from a tumbler he had placed without a coaster on the Chippendale end table Russell had had appraised at ten thousand dollars. When he slouched out of the room to answer the call of nature, and Russell's half-open eyes were trained on the semi-clad body of a hermaphrodite on adult Pay-Per-View—no doubt a product of the sheerest artifice—I slipped the straw from my pocket and emptied it into Apache's libation.

Half an hour later both he and Russell were sleeping like babies. I took advantage of the respite to make an exhaustive search of Apache's belongings, which he kept in a ragged army surplus duffel bag. There were threadbare undershirts, unclean socks with holes in their heels, an old towel, a pack of playing cards, a loaded and locked Glock semiautomatic, a utility knife, a T-shirt emblazoned with the legend "So what if I farted?", an unused stick of Old Spice deodorant, chewing tobacco, Q-tips in a less than pristine condition, and at long last, at the very bottom, a slim dime-store photograph album.

I opened it and flipped through the pages. The album contained pictures of only one person: a blond girl. The earliest snapshots featured her around the age of the three; the most recent, in my estimation, around the age of fourteen. Always thorough, I slipped each one out of its casing, searching for a clue to her identity. The closest I came was a childish scrawl that read, "Love U Daddy."

Carefully restuffing the bag, I moved next to his safari jacket, which hung beside him on the arm of the chair. He had taken to walking around the house bare-chested, allowing a full view of his pocked and scarred torso. (One nipple had been lopped off in the Crimea.) I knelt down and stealthily searched the pockets. His wallet, to my delight, held an additional picture of his daughter. On the back it said, "Chrissy."

I was still lacking vital information. I took his keys and went outside and down the block to the truck. In the glove compartment

I found a dog-eared address book. There was no Chrissy listed under his last name, but since there were only four people, total, in the address book, I had no trouble singling her out. Under the *P*s I found one address labeled simply "C," with a telephone number in Louisiana. When I called the number and asked for Chrissy, the woman on the other end said, "She's asleep, whaddaya think? And who the fuck are you to call this late?"

I ad-libbed and said I was Apache's girlfriend.

"Yeah? You tell that mofucker to stay the hell away from Chrissy and me."

The next day, around the time that my lunch hour began, Apache received a call from a nurse at a Baton Rouge hospital. Chrissy was very, very ill and was asking for him. Her mother had told the nurse not to call, but she was so moved by Chrissy's plea that she took matters into her own hands. Given the urgency.

According to Russell, who told me about it drowsily when I got home with a brand new box of Krispy Kremes, Apache had peeled out before three.

UNDONE

DAPHNE GOTTLIEB

When San Francisco Mayor Gavin Newsom (whom we tried to keep out of office with all our hearts) spurned national law and declared that San Francisco would issue marriage licenses, I was living with my _____. We were nothing if not a same-sex couple. She was my _____. I write _____ because, after being with her for nine years, living together for six, she was hardly my girlfriend, and much more than my lover; she was not my "significant other" and not my "partner," thank you. She was my (love). And if legally she had to be my "domestic partner" —if that was the only option we had, so be it. But domesticity does not rend buildings to the ground. Love does. She really was my _____ (love).

It was a few days shy of our nine-year anniversary, the leather anniversary according to Chicago's Public Library. We'd been together for all but five years of what I consider my "adult" life, if you start counting at twenty-one.*

We were deadlocked, trying to decide whether to go get married or not. It was like trying to decide whether to go get expensive sushi or not. Or buy a new sex toy we might not like. Actually, it was not like that at all.

We were going through a rocky period; a relationship mood swing. It was the kind not unfamiliar to anyone who has been in a relationship that has lasted more than two years recognizes as transient. Even so, each time you think, "Uh oh. It's over."

We went back and forth on the marriage thing: Oh yes. Oh no. Uh oh. We fretted privately and together. Marriage was important. Marriage was assimilationist. This was an important historical moment. This was tokenism.

The fact is, we'd had this conversation many times over nine years. And we'd decided that commitment ceremonies, though they can be really swell, weren't for us. They lacked any real legal reason to spend that kind of money—limos but no power of attorney, flowers but no bulletproof custody, champagne but no tax break, no deal. Not our kind of spending. Despite excited exhortation by some friends and enthusiastic hints from parents and sib-

_____

* Which I think is generous. There was someone I met before I turned twenty-one with whom I pledged to spend the rest of my life. It would have worked out, had I died at twenty-two. I think it's a common phenomenon. At least five in ten. Do you really want what you want at twenty-one to be what you want at forty-one? Not me. Even if it's the same person, maybe you want different things.

lings, we had demurred for almost nine years. We slyly told them we'd prefer to live in sin. After all, that's exactly what my mother proposed to my father, albeit under different circumstances.*

So. My _____ and I were choosing to live in sin, sort of. I chose to not suburb this, not soft-pedal this, not palliate this, not "my roommate" this. Because she was my wife, I called her, for a while, my "wife." Which was a grand political statement and a love letter all in one. Until we could actually get married.

And then there it was: our anniversary, Valentine's Day, and now we could be, like, legit. Obviously, I needed strong ammunition. I took aim at her hatred of tradition. "Oh, no," I said. "I'm not going to marry you unless you get down on one knee and propose." We both laughed, and I thought it was over. I breathed a deep sigh. And then she, who I had seen over nine years in sickness and health, who I had seen richer and poorer, shocked the shit out of me.

She got down on one knee and took my hands in hers.

"Do you remember," she said, "the early days of Queer Nation?"

Yes, I said, I did.

"Do you remember," she asked, "going into malls for kiss-ins and asking straight girls if they wanted to make a statement?"

Yes, I said, of course I did.

"And," she asked, if they said 'yes'," she said, "you'd kiss them?"

---

* They'd been married more than twenty years. He was dying. Living in sin seemed good enough for me if it was good enough for them. Of course, the last time they tried to have sex, the Jehovah's Witnesses interrupted them, but I can hope for better. Or maybe laughing is just fine.

Yes, I said. I remembered. "If," she said, "you want to make a statement with me, I would love to make a statement with you."

The world stopped for a minute.

"So," she said. "Do you want to make a statement?"

"I don't know," I said. I'm not sure how long I was crying for. Only that I wasn't crying alone.

Later that night I called my brother, an attorney in Los Angeles. "You know what's happening in San Francisco," I said. "This round probably won't hold up," he said. "I know," I said. But I might get married anyway." I explained the best reason for getting married I'd heard, the one that had convinced me: The courts would soon put a stop to these marriages, but there were couples all over the country who wished to get married and could not be in San Francisco for reasons of privilege of one sort or another—money, safety, and otherwise. We should, the argument went, get married on their behalf. Represent them in the statistics taken. We should do it for those who couldn't. My brother listened then laughed. "You do realize," he said, "that these are just about the only circumstances under which I can see you getting married."

At some point, though, here's what happened. We cried more. The cat got off the table. A few dinners got made. The TV went off and on and we went to work and slept and kissed, the real and warm of her mouth against mine making me realize something. I wanted marriage to mean something beyond resistance. I wanted my wedding, our marriage, if we chose it, to be the celebration and the pledge of fusing two lives together. I didn't want my wedding to be a test case. I want promises made in love to mean more than litigation.

There are photos of me at the age of five or so, wearing a veil and a wedding dress, playing dress-up. Not so many years ago, this was good training for the best a girl could expect from her life. For some, maybe that's still true. And though my mother wished desperately for me to choose the doctor costume first, the bridal getup had the better hat.

For me, the expectation of marriage was something so deeply ingrained early on that no matter my fear, dislike, and critique of it as an adult, the promises of a happily-ever-afterness still sing in my cells once in a while. And I'm ashamed to admit this. Because it feels shallow to me, like getting hot to mainstream porn, like wanting something from Old Navy even though you know it was made in a sweatshop, like somehow being the same as everything you thought you'd spent your whole life fighting against.

The truth is, I was never married. But I have been divorced. Even though all that I can correctly say is, "We split up." If I had said "divorced," maybe co-workers would have looked at me differently when I crept in late to work, red-eyed and suddenly stumbling, heaving-chested to the bathroom. Or when I didn't come in at all. I don't know that their opinions were any different than if I'd been married to a man. I really have no way of knowing.

She took the apartment. We split up the cats. She took a sublet. I found a roommate, found an apartment. We tore our lives, our hearts, apart and then I called her sobbing: I'd had to sign a form at work to end her healthcare. The form said, "Termination of Domestic Partnership." I called her through a choked throat, tried to explain. She tried to make it better. We hung up.

And then the certified letter arrived at her door, notarized. Not even needing her signature. In Saudi Arabia, it used to be possible to get a divorce by saying "I divorce you" three times. All it takes in America now, if you're queer and a registered domestic partner, is a notarized signature. If you're not registered, it takes even less.

I have never written marriage vows. Here are, belatedly, my divorce vows. My dear _____, who shared my heart for nine years, who will be in a part of my heart always: maybe, regardless what happens, there was a special love, a special fight in having had to get the power of attorney, to garner the domestic partner status through two different agencies, to correct the "roommate" slips, to have written the next-of-kin name in on forms with no legal protection. I jumped through these hoops with you, and I regret that our forever came sooner than the oldest ages we could reach. If there ever was a marriage vow I could give you, could have given you, it is this: I wish for your happiness every night as fervently as I wish for my own.

And, should your new someday love lead you that way, I hope you'll invite me to your wedding.

WOMB SHELTER

JONATHAN AMES

Yesterday, I was watching the girls play tennis.

I was trying to catch glimpses of panties beneath the little skirts.

Meanwhile, bombs were being dropped in Afghanistan. But the girls were still trying. Serving, running, volleying. Bending over. Yeah. Bend over. When I was fifteen I'd be alone in my basement watching Chris Everett on the television, my hands in my pants, waiting for her to bend over.

I also liked Tracy Austin's ass and Evonne Goolagong's. What a name. Goolagong. I think she might have been an Aborigine. You know she had a sweet pussy. A brunette pussy. I wish I could lick it right now. Even if she's fifty. To hell with writing. I'd like to lick Evonne Goolagong's pussy right now!

Anyway, the girls were playing. Six courts. Twelve girls. End-of-the-day fall light. Very pretty. Clean air. College! Hope! Young people! Flyers on bulletin boards! Go, tennis team! Blond ponytails. Long legs. Smooth legs. Twelve sweet pussies hidden somewhere in those skirts. Lots of bending over. Bombs dropping.

I was getting this delicious display of young bottom because I'm Writer-in-Residence for a month at this all-girls college. It's deep in the South. They have me up on a hill in a house, behind some trees, hidden. Like Anthony Perkins in *Psycho*. Down below is the soccer field and the tennis courts.

The tennis match was against Sweet-Briar-Fur-Patch College, and I have to say those girls were blonder, richer, classier. You could see it in their strokes. Their sneers. Oh, to have one of them in bed. This thin blonde with a good net game comes to mind. She was wearing glasses! Glasses on a girl can be very sexy.

One time, years ago, late at night on Rue St. Denis in Paris, which is lined with hundreds of whores (it's legal in Paris), I wasn't tempted by any of the women. I enjoyed looking—it was fun, sure—but I was impervious; wasn't going to waste my money, wasn't going to risk getting crabs or who knows what, even with a condom. So I watched the parade of my fellow men. The lonely suckers. There were probably a thousand men marching up and down the street for three hundred hookers. I was in the parade, but I was above it all. A voyeur. A writer observing life!

Then I saw this one wearing glasses. That did it. Had to have her. She was dark-haired and short. A sexy body. Full tits. A pretty face. But it was those cat-shaped black glasses. Oh, those glasses.

So we climb three flights to her horrible room. Low ceiling. Slanted floor. Walls so thin you could trace a drawing; something like that. The room had seen too much sad fucking. I gave her the money. She told me to undress. I did what she told me. Then she washed my cock with a wet rag. Probably spread diseases on it. Anthrax. Put anthrax on my cock. Wait, this was 1989. That wasn't popular back then.

After the cock cleaning, she undressed. Her body all trussed up in bra and girdle and hoses and clamps and hidden steel beams came melting out. Tits all dead. A Caesarian scar and stretch marks on her belly. But I had already paid. She yanked my thing to life and put a condom on it. We lay down. I caught a glimpse of her bush underneath a roll of fat. She took her glasses off, remembering at the last moment, and put them on the little night table. No! I could handle the scar, the fat, the yanking, but I needed those glasses for my hard-on.

But I was too embarrassed to ask. I was young then. Now I know to ask for what I need. Especially when it comes to the hard-on. I deflated, but she grabbed my soft thing and got it in her. She gave a couple of fake moans and kicked her heels in my ass like a jockey. I squeezed a boob and pinched a tired brown nipple. I put my mouth on the nipple and it hardened. This little spark of real life from her, even if involuntary, made me get hard, and when I got hard I came. It had lasted sixty seconds. I looked at the glasses on the night table. There's nothing worse than bad sex. Except bad sex that you've paid for. If only she had kept the glasses on.

Anyway, the blonde from Fur Patch College. She had glasses. Thin gold frames. If I had her here in my little house on the hill right now, I'd take her from behind. That tennis lesson ass would intuitively push back for more. Yes, sweet girl. Push back for it.

You sweet beautiful girl. I forgive you your sneer because you're a doll in bed.

Look over your shoulder at me with those glasses. You dear thing. You're wearing glasses but you're on your belly with your gorgeous ass in the air and your puss taking me in. You're a beautiful female animal. We're playacting at making babies. I love you!

Anyway, these Sweet-Briar-Fur-Patch girls were beating my girls pretty handily. Wouldn't you know I end up at a poor man's all-girls college. But what the hell. Better to be here than not to be here. An all-girls college feels like a pretty safe place as we go to war.

I only reported here for duty two days ago. They needed a writer at the last minute. Well, a month ago. But for academia, that's the last minute. Somebody recommended me, and so they hired me without reading my books. They only read the résumé, which looks good: Leon David, Yale '86, three novels. But they should have read the novels before letting me down here. I took the job because it's a one-liner for my friends. "I'm spending a month as writer-in-residence at this all-girls school." Gave everybody a laugh.

But I don't know if it's a laugh. I've masturbated nine times in forty-eight hours. That's way too much at my age, three years shy of forty. I look like I have two black eyes. I'm losing too much semen. All my nutrients are going out my cock. To hell with Afghanistan, I need the government to drop some food on *me*. Drop it on my cock. I'm so horny because I'm Jewish. Jews know their life is in danger all the time, that's why we're so horny. It's distasteful. We're about to get it in the neck again, I'm sure. I think Jews must have alien blood in them. Some alien screwed a sexy Jewess in the dessert five thousand years ago. That's why we're hated. We're part alien. How else do you explain Einstein, Freud, Gershwin, and Lewinsky?

If Lewinsky hadn't been so horny and brainy, she never could have sucked Clinton's cock. Granted, he was a fairly easy target, but still, it took a lot of brains and chutzpah and sex drive to give the president of the United States a blowjob. She's the Einstein of sex. And if he hadn't been dealing with his blowjob impeachment, maybe he could have done something in the Middle East and we wouldn't be going crazy right now bombing and getting bombed.

Well, it's all too much for me. And now it's lunchtime. I've been writing for two hours, imagining Goolagong's pussy and remembering that French pussy and wanting that Fur Patch girl's pussy. So I'm going to the dining hall where I'll be surrounded by six hundred real vaginas. Not imaginary. Real. Delicious. Beautiful. All being sat on while the girls eat. Incredible. I'm in a womb shelter. Bring on the bombs.

FEAR AND LOATHING
IN CHELSEA

ERIC ORNER

FEAR AND LOATHING IN CHELSEA

BY ERIC ORNER

THIRTY SUMMERS AGO I WAS AT CAMP PETOSKEY. WE WERE HAVING A COOKOUT ON SOUTH MANITOU ISLAND, AT THE VERY TOP OF LAKE MICHIGAN...

I WAS ENJOYING MYSELF—SORT OF BLISSED OUT ON THE BEAUTIFUL SUNSET, AND THE PROMISE OF HOT DOGS FOR DINNER; AND THE SWEET EXHAUSTION OF HAVING HIKED AND SWUM AND SAILED ALL DAY.

109

FEAR AND LOATHING IN CHELSEA

THE SUNSET WAS CASTING THIS WEIRD ROSY LIGHT...

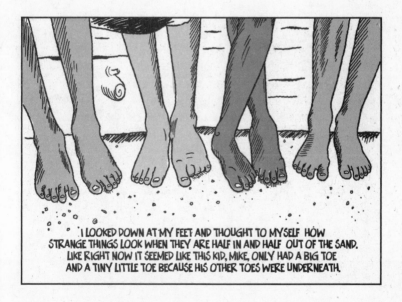

I LOOKED DOWN AT MY FEET AND THOUGHT TO MYSELF HOW STRANGE THINGS LOOK WHEN THEY ARE HALF IN AND HALF OUT OF THE SAND. LIKE RIGHT NOW IT SEEMED LIKE THIS KID, MIKE, ONLY HAD A BIG TOE AND A TINY LITTLE TOE BECAUSE HIS OTHER TOES WERE UNDERNEATH.

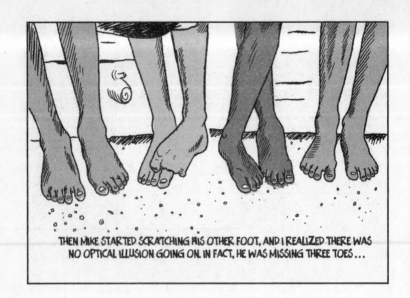

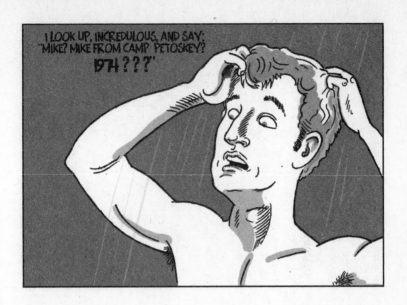

FEAR AND LOATHING IN CHELSEA

MEASURE A, B, OR ME?

ALISON TYLER

"Look at this, Lisa," James said, pointing to the voter registry spread out on his side of the kitchen table.

"Nice," I said, not glancing up from the newspaper.

"No, look right here." He tapped the middle of one of the pages.

I gazed at him over the top of my glasses. I was busy reading Dear Abby. James knows better than to interrupt me during Dear Abby.

"These two names," James insisted. With a sigh, I put down the paper and glanced where he was pointing.

"So? They have to list husbands and wives separately. Husbands don't own wives anymore, you know."

"I understand that you have zero interest in politics," James said in that calm voice of his, "but look at the parties."

Knowing James wasn't going to stop, I set down my coffee, stood up, and headed around to his side of the table. James had volunteered to phone registered voters to discuss a ballot measure close to his heart. And for the first time since he'd begun to talk incessantly about Ballot Measure A, I found myself interested in the cause, or at least mildly so. Here was personal information for nearly a quarter of the people in our tiny town. The list contained not only their names, numbers, and addresses but also their chosen political parties. A couple we knew ever so vaguely were registered with different parties—the wife a Democrat, the husband a Republican.

"How can that happen?" I asked curiously. "That was one of the first things I found out about you. Your religious preference, the size of your cock, and your political leanings. This is like something right out of a Dear Abby column."

"I don't understand it, either," James admitted, "but look at the governor and his wife, and there are other famous couples who vote on different party lines, too."

"You mean like Marlee Matlin and George Carlin?"

James groaned. "It's *Mary Matalin* and *James Carville*."

"Yeah, but how can they get into the same bed at night? I'd never be able to fuck you if I thought you were Republican. That would be an instant deal-breaker."

"More so than the size of my cock?" James teased, and while I was considering my answer, he continued, "Hey, let's have some fun."

Since James had embarked upon this mission to make sure Measure A passed, he'd been neglecting some of his more important husbandly duties. I'm not the type to care about whether the lawn is mowed or the car is washed. But I'd gone through three packs of C batteries for my vibrator in two months. Still, I didn't want to get my hopes up too high. "I thought you had people to call," I said tentatively.

"I'm *talking* about calling."

I sighed again. "Come on, James." I'd been hoping for a bit of frisky mid-morning fun. Dialing up voters wasn't my idea of kinky sex play. But I should have looked more clearly into my husband's deep blue eyes before writing him off.

"Lisa," he said in that patently annoying tone of voice, "I know you have zero interest in politics—"

"I'm a registered Democrat," I reminded him. "I wear my Stewart/Colbert '08 shirt every time I go to the gym. I have a 'Somewhere in Texas a Village Is Missing Its Idiot' bumper sticker on my Prius and a 'Don't Blame Me, I Voted for Kerry' button on my denim jacket. What more do you want?"

"Yeah," he nodded, "But you're not exactly involved. You'd rather watch *Friends* reruns than stand outside the Palace Market and register voters."

I shrugged.

"But you *could* be involved. What if you call the man and I call the woman. You'll be your charming little self and try to win him over to the cause, and I'll do the same with her. It'll be like a contest."

"That's not really fair. You don't *have* to win her over. She's *already* a Democrat. Besides, I don't have any idea what to say."

James glared at me, his nearly endless supply of patience finally waning. "Haven't you been listening to me make the last hundred forty-five calls?"

I nodded, lying. I tended to tune out as soon as I heard him say the words "This is James Miller, and I'd like to talk to you about Measure A."

"You just coo the same info to the man."

I looked at him for a moment. "What do I win if I get him onto our side?"

"You name it."

I motioned for him to dial. I could think of several propositions I was extremely interested in winning him over to—and not one on the current ballot. There was the up-against-the-wall position, of which I was fully in favor. And the bent-over-the-arm-of-the-sofa position, which I could fully support.

I could tell that James didn't think I'd go through with the bet. When he handed the phone to me for my turn, I pressed redial, asked to speak to Leonard Carson, then tried my best to explain the terms of the measure to the husband. Unfortunately, the jerk hung up the phone on me as soon as he realized where I was headed with my political speech.

"Well, *that* was successful," James said. "You didn't even try."

"You never know," I countered, "I'll bet they're talking about the issue right now."

"You think?" he asked.

"Yeah." I sat down on his lap. "She's saying, 'It's a good cause, Lenny.'"

"His name is Leonard."

"Sure, but she probably has a pet name for him. 'It's money for the schools.'"

James interrupted me again, "And he's saying, 'We sent our kids to private schools over the hill. What the fuck do we care about those rats in the public system?'"

"Why is he swearing?" I asked.

"Because he's an asshole."

"Just because he has a different viewpoint from you?"

"*You're* the one who said you'd never fuck a Republican," James pointed out.

I ignored him. "He's saying, 'Convince me.' And she's going on her knees on their expensive Spanish-tiled floor . . ."

"She's *not* going to give him a blow job over Measure A," James insisted.

"How do you know?"

"Would you?"

"Maybe she's more political than I am. You know I have zero interest . . ."

"So she's giving him one hell of a blow job. How's *that* convincing him to vote the way she wants?"

"Maybe you're right. She needs her mouth free to win him over." I hesitated, trying my best to envision the scenario. "Okay, they're in the kitchen, and she bends over the table, like this, and lifts her nightgown."

I demonstrated for James, sliding my short satin nightie to my waist. James eyed me for a moment, then got behind me. He ran his large hands over my panty-clad ass before pulling my knickers along my thighs. I shivered at his touch. It had been so long since he'd last stroked me like that. When he slipped his drawstring pj's down and pressed his body against me, I could feel how hard his cock was.

Cautiously, James slid a hand under my body and touched my pussy. "You're wet," he said. "Does talking about politics turn you on?"

"You know it," I told him, stifling a giggle. Even after he slid inside of me, he wouldn't stop taunting me.

"So, in your little fantasy, the wife says, 'Vote for Measure A and I'll let you fuck me'?"

"That sounds silly when you say it."

"It's beyond silly," James insisted. He continued to drive inside of me, working a little faster now. "They're not having a conversation like this at all. If anything, they're having some huge four-star fight because she's voting one way and he's insisting on voting the other. In fact, I'll bet he's saying, 'If you vote for Measure A, I'm going to have to give you a spanking.'"

That caught me off-guard, and for a moment I actually considered switching over to the dark side. But I still didn't want to give in. "Well, what if she says, 'You can do that thing you want to do'?"

"*What* thing?"

"You *know* what thing," I said coyly. "The thing you always want to, and the thing I hardly ever say yes to."

James was silent, but I knew he understood what I meant. "You'll let me do *that* if I vote for Measure A?"

"She's thinking about it."

"She?" he asked softly, "Or you?"

"I'm *already* voting for Measure A."

"You know what I mean."

"Yes," I said. "She's thinking about it, and *I'm* thinking about it—"

That was all James needed to hear. There was a tub of margarine still out on the table, and he leaned over and scooped out a fingerful. In seconds, he had lubed me up between my rear cheeks, his firm hands spreading me wide open. I shut my eyes and gripped even tighter onto the edge of the table, breathless.

James went slow at first, sliding his cock forward inch by inch, pressing hard, but not forcing. "Relax," he said.

"How can I relax when you won't vote for Measure A?"

"It's that important to you?"

James slipped in a little more, and I groaned. The sensation of being filled was almost overwhelming. Still, I somehow managed to reply. "Yes," I muttered. "Yes, it is."

Now he was fucking me even harder, gripping onto my slim hips and really driving his cock inside of me. My pussy was pressed firmly to the edge of the table, and through the filmy barrier of my nightgown, my clit received the most perfect pressure. I gasped as the rhythm of his thrusts increased in tempo, finding pleasure each time he slammed forward. I could come like this if he kept up the speed.

"You know," he said, "Measure A needs two yeses to counter every one no."

"Yes," I panted. "Yes, Yes . . ."

"That's three yeses," James said. "You can't vote three times." His voice had dropped to a whisper.

"Oh, god," I whimpered, unsure of what we were talking about or who I was. Was I Catherine trying to convince her bastard of a husband to vote yes on the school measure and help the children? Or was I Lisa, whose husband was already an activist, such an activist that he'd forgotten to take care of me for the past two months.

I squeezed my eyes shut even tighter as James slid one hand under my body and began to tap his fingertips against my clit. He knew exactly how to work me, thrusting forward with his cock, then giving me a little tap before slowly withdrawing. When he pinched my clit hard, I found myself teetering on the brink, hardly able to breathe until the climax finally flared through me. James let those powerful shudders transfer from my body to his, and then he groaned and began to work me even more seriously, before coming ferociously into my ass and sealing his body to mine.

It took me a moment to recover. The morning sunlight played over our sparkly blue Formica breakfast table. The tub of yellow margarine seemed to be mocking me.

James pulled out and tucked himself back into his pajamas. "I've still got twenty more calls to make," he said.

So he knew what was on his morning agenda, but I couldn't figure out what to do next. Dear Abby held no interest. Nor did finishing the rest of the paper. I wondered what Catherine and Leonard were doing right now. Was she bent over their kitchen table as I'd described?

Quickly, I slid my panties back up, then climbed onto my husband's lap once more. I pointed to the next Republican on the list. "If I can get her to vote for A, you let me do that to *you*." I told James.

He cocked an eyebrow at me, then pushed the phone over to me.

THE CANDIDATE'S WIFE

JAMES FREY

Jack and Dan sit at a bar in D.C. It's a dive bar in a declining neighborhood, a neighborhood that did not benefit in any way from the recent real-estate boom. Jack and Dan are both in their early thirties. Jack is a science teacher at a low-income public high school. Dan is an aide for a Democratic senator. They both grew up in Baltimore, have been friends their entire lives, went to elementary, middle, and high school together, went to college together. Both are from lower-middle class families and had to work their way through, Jack in one of the schools' cafeterias, Dan on a maintenance crew. When they finished, they got an apartment together in D.C, a two-bedroom in a crumbling brick building. They have been living in the apartment for the last six years. Until of one them gets married, which will not be anytime soon, they will continue to live there.

They come to the bar most nights. Sit and watch baseball or basketball and nurse beers. They check out whatever women are in the bar, sometimes they approach them, occasionally one of them gets into bed with one of the women. Both are good-looking men. Jack is tall and lithe. He has blue eyes and black hair. Dan is slightly shorter, heavier because he lifts weights three times a week, brown hair, brown eyes. Neither of them has ever had trouble attracting women. Together it's fairly easy.

It's a quiet night. The bar is almost empty, the Wizards are on TV; they're getting trounced by LeBron James and the Cavs. Dan has been working overtime for the last several weeks preparing for the midterm elections, which are a month away. His boss is not up for reelection, but he and his staff lend support to other Democrats who are, and everyone in his office is overworked. Away from the office, he avoids talking about politics. With Jack, there's no reason. Both are unabashedly liberal. They are pro-choice, anti-war, in favor of gun control, against budget cuts in education; both believe higher taxes can be used to make the country, and the world, a better place. Tonight they talk football. Despite being from Baltimore, they hate the Ravens, who are a new team and not part of the fabric of the city they grew up in, and love the Redskins. Jack speaks.

Portis is a bum.

Dan speaks.

He's great when he plays,

But he's not playing.

He's hurt. Football players get hurt sometimes.

He blew our season with that injury.

The season was blown already. We don't have a quarterback, and our defense sucks.

They'd both be better if Portis was playing.

You can't blame everything on Portis.

Yes I can.

I doubt he wanted to get hurt.

I bet he did.

Dan laughs.

You think he purposely ran into the three-hundred-thirty-pound-pound lineman who picked him up and slammed him to the ground thereby separating his shoulder and requiring reconstructive surgery?

Jack laughs.

Yes. I do.

They both laugh. The door of the bar opens. An attractive blonde woman in her early forties' walks in. Dan glances at her in the mirror behind the bar. He starts to say something to Jack, looks back into the mirror, watches the woman walk to a table in the corner and sit down. He turns around, gets a better look, turns back to Jack, speaks.

That's Susanne Carter?

So what.

You know who she is?

Middle-age blonde who was smoking hot nine years ago and is doing her best to age gracefully?

She's Thomas Carter's wife.

The senator?

Yeah.

No way.

It's her.

Why would the wife of a U.S. senator be in this shithole?

No idea.

It's not her.

It is.

Go talk to her.

What do I say?

Tell her you're an admirer of her husband.

Dan laughs.

Yeah, right.

Tell her you like her highlights, that the blonde streaks are subtle and disarming.

That's a good line.

Ask her if she wants a drink.

He motions towards her table, where a waitress is sitting down a cocktail glass.

Looks like she got one already.

Just go ask her if she wants to fuck.

She smiles and says yes; they end up in the men's room. It's small and cramped; it has a toilet and a urinal and a sink squeezed into a space the size of a closet. He presses her against the door their tongues in each other's mouths, pushing, tangling their hands grabbing, seeking one of his in her shirt the other up her skirt spreading both of hers are working the buttons on his pants. He unbuttons her shirt unhooks her bra starts sucking and biting. She drops his pants to the floor she pulls his head away from her chest and gets down on her knees.

She comes back the next night. He bends her over and her head hits the door with every stroke.

She's missing over the weekend, comes back on Monday. He sits on top of the toilet and she rides him while he sucks on her tits.

He takes her outside on Wednesday, they go into an alley behind the bar. She wraps her legs around his waist and he takes her against the wall.

Thursday they get into the backseat of her car. He goes down on her and stays down on her for forty-five minutes. He uses his lips, tongue, and fingers, uses them to give her a taste of herself. When he's done, he mounts her and gives her a taste of himself.

They do not speak to each other. They have never exchanged names or numbers. She just shows up and smiles and takes him by the hand and tells him what she wants.

She disappears for a couple weeks. Dan misses her, misses her smell and her taste, her hands, lips, and tongue, misses being inside of her. He watches the news and the papers and looks her up online, finds out that she's with her husband, who has gone back to his home state to campaign. He is running for his third term in the Senate. He is a conservative who serves a conservative state, a born-again Christian who is anti-abortion, pro-gun, supports the war in Iraq, and supports the idea of future aggression in the Middle East. He believes in creationism and prayer in public schools, believes that homosexuality is a curable disease and that all gays and non-Christians will burn in hell for eternity upon their death. His opponent is a moderate and has absolutely no chance of winning. Despite this, the senator raised a huge campaign fund and has run hundreds of ads on television, on the radio, and in newspapers, attacking everything from his hair and clothing to his wife, children, and marriage. The senator's justification for the ads is—God is going to judge him someday, I might as well do it now.

Jack and Dan sit at the bar. They're both drinking beer. Jack speaks.

Have you told her what you do?

Dan speaks.

No.

You think you should?

No.

Why not?

Because we never talk. And because it's irrelevant.

You really think that?

Yeah.

If her husband was a mortgage broker or an insurance agent, would you be fucking her?

No.

Would you have even approached her?

No.

Then it's relevant.

Maybe to me, but not to her.

How about her husband?

It's probably very relevant to him. For a number of reasons.

She shows up the next night. Dan's surprised because he knows her husband is having a debate with an opponent. He's sitting at the bar; she comes up behind, whispers, let's go fuck, in his ear.

They leave. Get in her car. He wants to get a motel room; he starts driving. She gives him head as he drives. When they find a motel, they park and she finishes him off. He gets out, goes into the lobby, gets a room. As he walks to the room, she gets out of the car and follows him into the room. He closes the door and she's on him. They fuck twice; the second time he takes her anally. When they're done they lie in bed. Her head rests on his chest. There is a streak of light coming through a crack in the curtains. He speaks.

You've never told me your name.

She speaks.

Is there some reason you need to know it?

It would be nice to put a name to your face.

My face?

Among other things.

My name is Jane.

Jane what?

Jane Doe.

He laughs.

You think that's funny?

Sort of.

It's not, not at all, and it wasn't supposed to be a joke.

Okay.

It's important to me that you know me as Jane Doe. I fuck you. I suck your cock. I let you do whatever you want to me. I'll keep doing it as long as you acknowledge me as Jane Doe.

I can't do that.

Why?

I work on the Hill.

She sits up, stares at him. There is shock and rage in her eyes, spreading across her face.

You work on the fucking Hill?

Yes.

What do you do?

I'm an aide to a Democratic senator.

She stares at him for a moment, gets up, puts on her clothes, walks out. When she's gone, he stands and spreads the curtain and watches her walk to her car and get inside her car and pull out of the parking lot.

Jack and Dan sit at the bar. They're both drinking beer. Jack speaks.

Are you surprised?

Dan speaks.

Yeah.

Why?

There was something there.

Jack laughs.

You spoke to her once.

So what.

So there couldn't have been much.

I love her.

Jack laughs again.

You're fucking kidding me.

Dan shakes his head.

I'm not. I love her.

You're never gonna see her again.

Probably not.

That's why you love her. That shit happens when you get dumped.
Doesn't matter if you loved the person or hated them, if they dump
you, you yearn for them and miss them and love them and feel all
the shit you didn't probably feel when you were with them. It's
stupid and crazy, but that's the way it is.

I know that syndrome well. It's not that.

What is it then?

If I knew it'd be easier. That's part of the problem. And it doesn't
matter that we hardly spoke. When we were together there was that
thing, that unexplainable thing, and I felt it, felt it very strongly.

And you think it's love.

I don't think. I know.

And it doesn't matter that she's married to the fucking Antichrist.

Nope.

And that she'll never leave him.

Nope.

You're fucked, dude.

Yeah.

Dan is walking to a meeting on the Hill. As he starts to climb the
stairs leading to the entrance, he notices there is a press conference
being held at the landing. There is a lectern set up; her husband is
standing in front of it. She is standing next to him. They are surrounded by aides and advisors. A large group of reporters stands
in front of them recording every movement, every word. Her husband is speaking passionately about the need for faith-based aid
and the effectiveness of evangelical charities. She is watching him,

nodding and clapping at the appropriate times, looks the model of a supportive wife. Dan stops when he reaches the crowd. He stares at her. She glances toward him, sees him, does not acknowledge him in any way. He knows she saw him, and recognized him; she continues smiling and clapping at the appropriate times. He stands and watches the rest of the press conference, including the question-and-answer session with the reporters. When it's finished he walks to his office. She walks away with her husband and their entourage.

He watches the returns on the day of the election. Her husband wins in a landslide.

Five months later. Jack and Dan sit at the bar. They're both drinking beer, watching the Nationals get crushed by the Mets. Jack speaks.

The Nationals suck.

Dan speaks.

Yeah.

You think they'll ever be any good?

No idea.

The door of the bar opens, she walks in. Dan sees her in the mirror. He smiles, watches her walk toward his stool; she's smiling. She stops behind him, whispers in his ear.

I've missed you.

He nods.

I tried to stay away but I couldn't.

He smiles.

I got a room at our favorite motel.

He turns around, stares at her. He stills feels it, whatever it is, still feels it strongly.

I want you to take me there and fuck me.

He stands, takes her by the hand. They walk out of the bar.

TRANSFIXED, HELPLESS, AND OUT OF CONTROL

Election Night 2004

CHARLIE ANDERS

Queerdom cries. The hot young things at Eighteenth and Castro gather around the world's suckiest television screen, made out of bedsheets and milk crates, watching the world turn red. "It's okay," people keep saying over and over again, "Ohio's still a toss-up." Over in the Midnight Sun, it's almost a relief when they show a Village People video instead of Dan Rather's folksy ramblings. Dan Rather says the election is as sticky as a squirrel in heat covered with forest burrs. He says John Kerry is as desperate as a nudist in a freak hailstorm.

Queer theory didn't prepare you for this, did it? Everywhere I look, tragedy strikes down Gay Shame and the Marriage Equality people alike. Even the Village People are not enough to rescue our crumbling psyches. Skinny fags and dykes in tight shirts and pants look as though someone just set fire to their gourmet dog biscuit store.

"But, but . . . I mean, Kerry won Maryland," this one girl says through tears and hair and maybe snot. She's normally kempt, but the election returns are challenging her kemptness. We're looking at the screens on the outside of the Midnight Sun, on the sidewalk. "That's good, isn't it? Maryland's in the South, sort of. He won a southern state." Seeing her so desperate, so miserable, so, so . . . achy for a promised reward, suddenly I'm all horny. She has that look, the one that bottoms get when you've promised them an orgasm if they'll just do one little thing for you, and then it turns out you lied.

I like that look. I go to great lengths to elicit it from my bottoms.

I will now cut and paste a paragraph from my last Craigslist ad, to avoid having to describe myself in this story. "I'm forty two years old, but can pass for forty-one. Been an SM dyke since the Iran-Contra scandal. Mostly bony but with some curves. Brown hair, brown eyes, fair skin. Leather-wearing femme. Sadistic and sarcastic, but not Socratic." There, now you've got a mental picture. Bully for you.

Before I've consciously thought about it, I've decided unkempt girl is my prey. She has latte-colored skin and long wavy hair. Turns out her name is Lexa and she's an MFA student at State. She's still crying over John-boy and his terrible shortfall. NBC has called Ohio for Bush, but everyone else is reserving judgment.

It's not looking good, is it? I ask her, not having to fake my own disappointment. It feels so useless to be standing around here, watching and waiting. I sigh theatrically.

"Yes, I feel so awful," Lexa says. "And yet, transfixed."

The way she says the word *transfixed* gets me all hot again. Don't ask me why, it just does. I want to transfix her.

Like a train wreck, I say. You want to look away, but you can't.

"Exactly," she says. "Helpless."

I have to bite my lip when she says that word. I sigh again, ostensibly at the election results. Yes, I say. But at times like this, it's good just to be close to another human. To feel alive. Do you know what I mean?

She says she does, but I know she doesn't. I chat with her some more: about the stupidity of the Electoral College, all those huge empty red states where nobody lives deciding who gets to be president, the gerrymandering of the House of Representatives, the corporate ownership of the media, does democracy even exist anymore? Blah blah blah. Paralysis seeps into her limbs, like bondage without any torture except for the slow death of hope.

I feel the need to rescue her from all this, to replace her mental anguish with another type of pain.

Don't get me wrong—I'm upset too. The thought of four more years of Bush, of Bush with a Mandate between his mandibles, fills me with creeping sickness. It's not just her I'm trying to rescue. My lust is a welcome distraction.

I whisper in her ear: it's late, there's nothing we can do here, they won't call the election tonight, there's still hope, why don't you come back to my place for some tea and cakes, we can keep an eye on the results from there. . . . She nods, slowly.

I live in Outer Noe Valley, past Lovejoy's Tea House. Tea and cakes are very important to me. They symbolize politeness, friendliness, companionship, stickiness—all good things. My apartment is sort of a Steampunk railway car, with a small dungeon area next to the computer, which looks piston-powered but isn't.

While Lexa is looking around with what I hope is a mixture of terror and admiration, I busy myself with scones and decaf Earl Grey. Clotted cream, strawberry jam. We must Keep Up Our Strength. Lexa is staring at the small but impressive bondage area: rings in the ceiling and floor, sling pinned up on one wall, an assortment of floggers and torture devices on a lacquered tray. The whole thing soundproofed with big tapestries, including one a friend gave me that shows the traditional unicorn getting ass-fucked by the virgin with a strap-on.

I make loud tea-serving noises behind her so she won't feel as though I'm sneaking up on her. I hand her a cup and saucer, gesture to the milk and sugar in their floral china homes. I touch her wrist and she nearly spills. This could be our last chance, I say. To enjoy life. Before the repression starts.

"Oh no," she says. "There's still hope. Maryland, I mean. And Ohio is a toss-up!"

Yes, yes. Always hope. And meanwhile, I offer her a scone, but she's not hungry. I ask her if she likes my bondage gear, and she says yes. Sometimes, I say, transgressive sex can be an act of resistance against hegemony. She likes that; I knew she would.

I put my hand on the back of her neck and she moans. Just a light touch. She's still holding the teacup, which keeps her from making any sudden movements. I run my fingers down her neck and along her shoulder, through her sweater. I finally take the tea away from her and put it down on the little table next to my computer. I come back to her—she hasn't moved—and I run my fingers over her cheek. She closes her eyes, goes into a mild trance. I keep stroking her cheek, run my other hand over her body without touching it. She can just feel my palm pass by her breasts, stomach, cunt, without touching.

I tell her to take off her sweater. It's an over-the-head thing that leaves her blinking and muss-haired. I stroke her lips with my finger and she opens her mouth to take it inside. I undo the clasp of her jeans with the other hand.

This could be our last night of freedom, I tell her. We have to be prepared for the worst. She's given up on contradicting me. Her jeans fall to the floor, bunched around her boots. Now she's just wearing an anti-globalization T-shirt, panties, and boots. I tell her to shout "red state" if I do anything she doesn't like. She nods.

I tell her to undo her boots and mine, to save time and to maximize the time she spends bent over. Her ass is even more amazing in panties than it was in jeans. It would make an excellent center of resistance; it could contain the revolution in its roundness. When she stands up again, I stroke her thighs with almost no pressure at all. She's a fun bottom, she twitches just from a little petting. Skittish.

You're lucky, I tell her. A pretty one. They'll keep you to breed the next generation of Jesus droolers. You'll learn to like reading the (and here I smack her left butt cheek) *Left Behind* books. You'll be a good fundy wife, in time.

She pushes her ass back to meet the spanking halfway. I swat too lightly to hurt, until she begs me to spank her harder. I pull her panties off, leaving her wearing just the T-shirt. I move her panties, jeans, socks, and boots out of the way, then guide her ankles to the rings in the walls of my little bondage cubbyhole. I put velcro cuffs around her ankles and snap them onto the rings. I leave her arms free, so she could free her ankles in seconds. But I know she won't, and this way her legs are spread nicely. I make her bend over slightly so I have a nice view of her ass and pussy.

Now that I'm sure she's not going to run away, I can commence the mindfuck in earnest. Oh, I mean it's not really a mindfuck, it's catharsis, it's helping her to confront the inevitable. Not really a mindfuck at all.

I spank her harder and tell her all the horrible things that will happen. Polluters will rewrite all the environmental regulations and pollute our wetlands. (Here I brush her own wetlands, just a little.) The FBI will place us all under surveillance in the name of Homeland Security. (Whap!) Antonin Scalia will be chief justice. (I claw her back under her T-shirt.) Abortion rights will wither. (Smack!)

I get my suede flogger and start on her ass and thighs. Perversely, I don't want to take off her T-shirt yet. You thought things were going to change? I say, giving her nice even strokes back and forth, mixed with little cooling touches. Well, they'll change, all right—you're going to learn what patriarchy's all about! Are you excited?

"No," she sobs. She's biting her lip to keep from crying. It's delicious; for a moment it's almost worth another four years of Junior. Almost. "No, I hate it."

I know, it's scary, I say. Do you want to feel nice for a while, to take your mind off it?

She nods and blinks. Now I pull her T-shirt up, but not all the way off. I leave it covering her head, so her arms are raised and she's blindfolded. I tell her not to move it. Then I start stroking her breasts, her sides, her armpits. Some of my touches make her purr and twist her body, others make her jump a little from ticklishness. She's lost in sensation.

Then I start in again, predicting. A few rich CEOs will control the entire economy, you'll be their slave. Your vegan boutiques will turn into Gap outlets. We'll turn the whole Middle East into a crater.

And so on. This whole time, I'm giving her little touches, licks, and bites on her thighs, breasts, stomach. I put a latex glove on one hand and lube up a finger. I smear lube around her ass and she moans louder, rotating her butt in supplication. I keep fingering and whispering in her T-shirt-covered ear.

They'll teach creationism in school, I murmur. They'll ban sex education and teach everyone that masturbation causes AIDS. My finger is pressing against her butt hole now. She pushes back. Pretty soon my finger is moving in and out and around, slicking her inside and out. She's bucking and gasping. They're going to round up the queers and put us in camps, I say. She wails.

I'm just getting warmed up. I keep finger-fucking her ass with my left hand and flogging her shoulder blades with my right hand. I can't flog too hard, because it's hard to coordinate and I don't want the flogger to wrap around accidentally. But it still stings. Pleasure below, pain above.

We're this close to a military dictatorship, I say, snapping the flogger against her shoulder blades. She squeals. All it takes is one little shove—I push my finger further into her ass—and we'll turn into real fascists. I work a second finger into her ass and she once again backs up to welcome it in. They'll suspend the Constitution and the Bill of Rights. I'm not even trying to be gentle anymore;

the fingers are thrusting and the T-shirted head and arms are flailing. The feds will strip-search you in the streets whenever they feel like it. They'll cavity-search you.

Somewhere inside the anti-globalization shirt, a little voice is begging, "No, no, no, no . . ."

I decide to check in. Are you doing okay? Are you ready to cry "red state" yet?

"I'm okay," she says between sobs. "Please don't stop."

That's all I needed to hear. Are you ready to be cavity-searched by Homeland Security? She cries and says "no" over and over again. I keep claiming her ass. Are you ready for Christian reeducation camps?

"No, no, no, no, no!"

I get a Baby Jesus butt plug and ease it into the opening I've made. I let her know that if she lets it fall out, I will leave her tied up and tell Tom DeLay where to find her. She whimpers like a puppy. The butt plug stays in. Good girl. I take off the glove.

I whip her tits, then finger her pussy, then whip her tits some more. I put a couple of Day-Glo clamps on her nipples and then whip her tits again, flicking them back and forth.

In the new world, women will be property, I hiss in her ear. You'll have to act like Laura Bush, stand behind your man.

My fingers circle around her clit. It trembles. Oh yes, you'll enjoy being Hester in our Puritan new world. I get a Hello Kitty vibrator and work her clit with it. I move closer to her clit every time I say something to upset her.

Bzzzz. . . . Hate crimes will become public policy. "Oh yes, please, yes!" Bible study will be mandatory. "Please, yes, please don't stop!" We'll all have to swear loyalty to Bush. "Yes, yes,

yes!" They'll have a curfew at night and all day Sunday except for church. "Oh god, more!"

Finally, just as I'm telling her that Congress will mandate public burnings of queer books, she screams as if it's her last breath, she shakes and flails and Baby Jesus flies out of her and she goes rigid and then collapses.

Ankles still cuffed, she leans against one wall, her body slack. Reality seeps back into her mind. All the things I said before unspool again, only this time without the thrill of bondage and arousal to soften them. She's left mostly naked, really helpless, in a terrifyingly ugly world. I ask her if she'd like to come back sometime soon, and she says yes.

A CRYSTAL FORMED
ENTIRELY OF HOLES

NICK FLYNN

1

At first it was just a kiss, tentative at first, her lips moving over his body, she found the hole, one of them, one that the AK-47 had left, this one in his bicep, her tongue fluttered over the wound, healed now, grazing it lightly, as if to say, *it's alright, I still want you, you're still beautiful*, and on the third pass her tongue slid in, at first just the tip, and he didn't push her away, and as her tongue went deeper he shuddered down to some untapped core and moaned and it surprised them both.

Word spread across the base. It was only a matter of time before it caught on.

2

In 2006 a physicist in Texas had synthesized a crystal formed entirely of holes. *A crystal formed entirely of holes.* You couldn't hold it in your hands, but its mass could be measured by how much air it displaced, by the way light passed through it. It came directly from research into the shape of nothing, which had been revealed to great fanfare a few months earlier, with charts and renderings and shadowy drawings.

3

As with most pure science, the military was the first to understand the practical applications—put bluntly, they had so many bodies shot through with so many holes, a simple, unavoidable by-product of their business. Bad enough, the casualties, but the injuries, the wounded—they never play well on TV. A military researcher read about the new crystal—what if one combined this nonentity, this synthetic nothing, with even rudimentary stem-cell technology—he speculated it could create, in essence, an entire new organ, the hole itself would become the organ—an evolutionary leap, but not the first—vegetables had been engineered for decades, every species from one-cell bacteria on up had by now been cloned. The higher-ups didn't care much about the Darwinian aspects to it, they were just tired of bleeding out. If it worked, the idea was to apply this new technology to those wounded in battle—shrapnel blows a hole through your skull, the wound itself becomes a new organ, incorporated into the body. If it worked—and there was every reason to believe it would—even a hand or a leg, blown off, could be restored. You still wouldn't be able to see it, but technically it wouldn't be classified as missing. Every soldier could now walk off a plane into his or her loved one's arms, for all the world to see. Home, waving a hand that wasn't there, the sun shining through the hole shot through his chest. Win-win.

4

A soldier lay in a dusty parking lot in Baghdad, a jagged line machine-gunned across her chest, holes that will kill her, holes through which her life will escape, unless these holes themselves can be incorporated into her body.

Stateside, six weeks later, at her bedside, her boyfriend pulls back the bedsheet to see how she's healing—seven pink-tinged, round-lipped blossoms. His finger hovers briefly over each one, tracing their swelling. She shudders, takes his face in her hands, and kisses him, their first real kiss since the operation, now pressing her whole body against him, rubbing the holes against his chest. He places his finger in his mouth, wets it, and circles the hole shot through her collarbone, slowly working his finger inside, below the surface, working it slowly in and out, making it bigger, slowly able to accept two fingers, then three.

By the end of the night he'd filled every one.

5

Erika watched the soldiers coming off the plane, waving their empty hands. Her mother was on the couch reading magazines called *"Us"* and *"InTouch,"* which Erika called *"Them"* and *"Out of Touch."* The air conditioner whirred to life. This was the apartment they'd lived in since her father vanished. Sunlight shone through a soldier's mouth. That's messed up, Erika said to no one, switching channels.

6

Side effects. As with everything, there's side effects. Once you're brought back from the other side, once you've gone over, you no longer recognize where you're from, not really—*you're a new freakin' species, soldier, what do you expect?* Still, you were shipped back to where you came from, shipped home. It was impossible for you to stay. Baghdad? Tikrit? For what? To wander the desert with a hole through your heart?

7

It wasn't exactly boredom—more a sense of the unreal. Houston, to Erika, felt deeply unreal, even if she couldn't point at anything specific and say, what *is* that? Everywhere she looked was another temple to the ultra-real—a coffee shop that smelled like coffee, a record shop lined with bins of used CDs. The tattoo on her backside, she'd wake some mornings, keep her eyes shut, trying to remember what it was. Flames? A snake? Three snakes entwined around something? What? Why did she get it? With who? What did it mean? Maybe it was a lotus blossom. She'd read somewhere that because of all the barbeque joints in Houston, the air over the city was made up of 10 percent burnt particles of flesh—*particulate matter*. Maybe she heard it on the radio—she could still hear a voice pronouncing the words *particulate matter*. She read somewhere else that the drinking water was 6 percent antidepressants, from sewer runoff seeping into the groundwater. *Pissing in a river, watch the fish smile.* Erika calls herself a vegetarian, some days. THE AIR IS MEAT, the graffiti on a bridge over 59 said—BE HAPPY.

8

The porn industry picked up the ball, first the low-end companies, the bucket shops, but it quickly spread to the mainstream. Click onto YouTube, type in "a crystal made entirely of holes," and you can see it, a video, homemade. It shows the tonguing, lots of tonguing, but it doesn't show how to make the holes.

9

Houston is the center of the plastic surgery world—more people alter themselves here than anywhere else on the planet. In Houston there's a plastic surgeon; let's call him Dr. Malick. For awhile Malick oversaw the coercive interrogation wing at the federal prison downtown. State-of-the-art facility, high-risk prisoners. With the passage of the Military Commissions Act, safeguards had been put in place to prevent the abuses and embarrassments of another Abu Ghraib. Strict oversight. In the interrogation rooms, Malick perfected a technique to simulate the effects of a shrapnel or bullet wound to flesh, and then he would "heal" the wound, a few moments or a few hours later, after the questions had been asked, after the answers had been given, or not given.

10

Word spread. The skateboard punks who used the concrete fortifications outside the prison as jump ramps heard about what was happening on the other side of the walls. They saw the nighttime deliveries—a hooded man, an orange jumpsuit, the spray-painted goggles, the old school headphones that silenced everything.

11

Malick opened the first Drive-Thru Holery in the desolation of downtown, out of a storefront below the Pierce Street overpass. He'd recently been retired from the prison—rumors he'd gone a little too far, though no formal charges were filed. Malick kept a running tally on an electronic billboard, visible from the highway, of the number of holes he'd "punched." YOUR MIND IS YOUR ONLY LIMIT! was the tag line. At first he gave out a Krispy Kreme to each customer—the perfect synergistic franchise—though now he doesn't bother. No one ate them anyway.

12

Once it caught on, Erika said it was all she'd found to believe in, that her god-given body had always seemed so limiting. Her god-given body filled her with despair, she said. It wasn't a matter of belief, because she professed to believe nothing. She and the other skateboard punks found themselves wanting more, more *options*. The flesh they were born with, the few holes they were given, the few ways they'd found to fill them, it wasn't enough, not anymore. Maybe it never was. They wanted some new organs. They wanted to be transformed, they wanted to become new freakin' species.

13

Maybe it was the Krispy Kremes, but after they got their first hole, the punks called themselves "donuts"—those with twelve called themselves "a dozen."

14

One hole per visit was allowed, by law, though there was no limit on the number of visits one could make. One could come every day—Erika came every day. *I'm a dozen*, Erika said, *I'm two dozen*. The day you got a donut someone else had to drive you home—that was the other rule. Those days Erika's boyfriend got the donut instead of her she'd drive away with one hand on the wheel and her other hand tearing off his bandage. Most days, though, she came alone. For Erika, Malick bent the rules—Saint Erika, pilgrims crossed the parking lot on their knees just to touch her toe, her toe with a hole shot through it.

15

Her body was state-of-the-art. You could see the sky through her forehead, the stars through her palm. Bones were rearranged; bones weren't a problem. She wanted each hole to shoot clean through to the other side, she wanted to shoot through to the other side. One more and she'd be gone. *Pure donut*, it was called, but no one had yet gone that far. A crystal made entirely of holes. Malick knew Erika would go that far, she was that beautiful. From that moment on, we'd only glimpse the outline of where she'd once been.

NOTES ON REDEVELOPMENT

RICK MOODY

Your honor, these are my introductory notes, and though I don't need to tell you, let me add that of course they are being composed against the backdrop of the secessionist movement here in our newly partitioned country. These notes are further to how we, as municipal executives, might redevelop the crumbling Giuliani Way and environs, the neighborhood formerly known as Times Square. That is, for the betterment of civic programs generally, with especial attention to the problem of diverting significant monies to the education budget and to the Abolishment of Homelessness Project, I do hereby propose the Pornography or Salacious Entertainments Relicensing Act (hereafter abbreviated POSER).

The first and most obvious point follows. Now that the voters of the Mid-Atlantic States, along with the New England region, have made the commitment to sunder ties with what was formerly known as the United States of America, we are no longer bound to observe restrictive federal statutes relating to tie-wearing, overt signs of belief or belief in the true and risen Christ, ankle-length dresses, and the necessity of reserving sexual congress for reproductive purposes.

Accordingly, as one of only four transgendered members of your administration, as a adventurer in the arenas of gender and human sexuality, I feel I am now in a unique position to recommend certain kinds of businesses that will attract to our city a great number of visitors (and tourist currencies) via the newly restored Port Authority Bus Terminal, the Bloomberg Heliport, the Forty-second Street Pier, Westway, and so forth. First, as you know, transgender businesses flourished in the area during the highly regarded period known as the First Great Decadence, and I would therefore like to propose some expansionist licensing along these thematic lines, such as the TV Makeover Hut, in which people are encouraged to stop into a storefront and have themselves made over, in particularly provocative ways, in the payment of opposite sex, whereupon they will be filmed (in the performance of exotic dances) by local webcasting operations. Since the female-to-male transvestite impulse has now become so commonplace as to be practically normal, it would be easy to promote such a business as especially family friendly. Off the record, I am more than capable as regards the solicitation of seed monies for any "trans-related" businesses.

Church-related sexuality has become very popular lately as well. We estimate seven or eight deconsecrated churches along

Giuliani Way, and these could easily be turned into businesses that cater to this very popular fetish. Orgies or one-on-one encounters on the altars of these churches, with voyeurs encouraged to pay for the right to serve as witness to these sessions, could be a hit. Moreover, returning to the transvestite and transgender imagery, it's obvious that many of the people who have led extremely constricted "heterosexual" lives during the theocratic governments of the early twenty-first century could now have the opportunity to wear the vestments of church attire to pursue their experimental sexual encounters. It is, these days, practically a superstitious belief that defiling a priest's cassock while making a baby out of wedlock will ensure the baby's longevity and his/her robust engagement in physical love in later life.

The amateur pornography studios that have begun turning up in Balkan and Central European pornographic markets in recent years have not been attempted here with the sort of marketing *oomph* that they really require, so I have an additional proposal along those lines. We all know that the old single-room occupancy hotels of the Midtown area served ably as sets for pornographic films, and we know that the more tawdry a pornographic film, the better its postprandial glow, so it should be possible to convert one or more of these dormant hotels back into "self-guiding pornographic production stations," where people who are above the reasonable new age of consent may feel free to film themselves performing the exercises of love with anyone who happens by, as long as these people or persons have had the de rigueur on-the-spot STD swabs. Imagine "self-guiding pornographic production stations," or SGPPSs, as common or easily accessible as automatic teller machines (ATMs). Again, there may be crossover revenue streams available to us here, especially in concert with the Office of Internet Projects, which is eager to license larger numbers of filmmaking operations in the city than we saw during and after the G-Rated-Only Family Film Act of 2012.

Recall if you will, your Honor, the Rev. Beauregard group-rape incident. We, as a legally chartered municipality, as one of the truly great international cities of the world, cannot publicly condone lawless vigilantism. We can decry the sort of poltroonery that leads young anarchistic toughs of our city to journey a thousand miles south and to imprison and violate the person of a leading southern theologian. But while we can oppose the original events, there is really no obstacle to promoting a business model based on quality-controlled public theatrical reenactments of the Rev. Beauregard group-rape incident. It would be, ergo, part of the Blows for Liberty campaign that has been so symbolically rich for the grass-roots campaigners of the northeastern secessionist movement. Who are we to stand in the way of this interpretation of the events? In fact, it would be possible to set up a sex-related Great Moments in American History theatrical extravaganza, perhaps on the site of the former Peep World Center, which was recently landmarked. In this venue, sexual tourists could have their way with various robotic likenesses of presidents, senators, and others from the annals of history. I think everybody agrees that sexual congress with presidents just helps regular folks let off steam, as it also alleviates stress and resentment about politics in general.

Slavery also offers us some opportunities, now that it is again being practiced in the southern states. There are whispers on the sexual theory circuit and in the sexual think tanks springing up at the better private universities in the city that ritual enslavement of southern people may help citizens of our region deal with the secession-era economic crises that continue to beset us. It is well known, of course, that monetizing a human life is *always* enticing. Women are especially enticing when monetized, now that they are trying even harder to balance professional life and new post-marriage single-parenting family models. As a woman who was formerly a man, my personal feeling is that enslavement helps women feel *more* powerful and *more* productive in the office, especially women in high-powered post-national corporate settings. These post-national corporations are uniquely situated to underwrite sexual slavery businesses, public auctions, etc., since these corporations operate above and beyond United Nations efforts to control human trafficking.

I suggest twenty-four-hour live slavery auctions on Giuliani Way, which could be conducted simultaneously on the Internet, where the bidding pools would be larger. Given our breakdown of relations with the southern and western parts of the former United States of America, it's obvious that women and fifteen-year-olds (here again taking advantage of the more practicable age of consent), and persons who are or resemble Baptists, Mormons, and other cult-oriented Magical Thinking Systems, would be especially prized at these auctions, when subjected to ritualized sexual humiliation of a family-friendly sort. While I'm not suggesting we kidnap such persons, as this would clearly cause diplomatic crises, we could easily make use of them in a slavery auction business, should they happen to attempt to slip across the border.

I also have an idea for a World's Fair of Perversion at some of the theaters of Giuliani Way. The model here is the old Disney "Small World" exhibit so well attended at those discredited theme parks. Now that the former United States of America is a third-rate economic power, a lapdog of the new China (I suppose we can in part blame the New Shepherding Movement that took hold in the South and West, which obviously didn't bring Jesus back any faster), we are already beginning to fetishize the sexual charge of the countries that are the powerhouses of the new age. In the World's Fair of Perversion, international visitors, with their all-important international currencies, would be able to sample the wares of local actors dressed as foreign dignitaries from these nations. I'll give you one example, just off the top of my head. Indonesia, that Asian economic miracle, was known in the past to punish boys who engaged in homosexual activity with dismemberment, after which the boys in question were devoured by the villagers. I suggest an Indonesian display in which we simulate group copulation with Indonesian nationals, after which we serve modest helpings of steak tartar.

Your honor, I'm well aware that POSER-related businesses could be construed by some as a little too novel even for our forward-thinking community. Maybe some among your estimable retinue of thirteen wives, for example, will consider them tasteless. If my suggestions are too excessive, we can just return to our earlier idea for all-pornography-all-the-time video billboards on Giuliani Way. Now that the entire outside of that ancient architectural masterpiece, the Time-Warner building, is being used as a video billboard for web-based broadcasts, it would of course be possible to have gigantic outdoor pornographic broadcasts wherein the relevant parts of the bodies of the actors and actresses would be so gargantuan and so realistic in their high-definition rendering that it would be difficult not to *swoon* over them. Who would not *want* such a thing, such a gigantic depiction of sexual *longeur*? Would it not stir up all their inert and melancholy molecules of the dispirited human body? And I don't need to tell you, your Honor, how gigantic broadcasts would give us opportunities for gigantic product placement.

Upon enacting any portion this legislation, we could then tax the resulting businesses liberally, as I have said. The revenues could then serve elsewhere. Health care, education, housing, pension insurance for employees public and private (in lieu of the abolishment of Social Security that took place in 2018), sex education, arts programming, etc. If you need anyone on staff to begin the process of sampling the buffet of Salacious Entertainments that might serve as anchor businesses, so that we might proceed with the campaign I'm outlining, let me be the first to volunteer.

PURPLE TULIP

TSAURAH LITZKY

I walk down a narrow, dirty alley smelling of piss, turn right, and I am in the heart of desire—the red-light district in Amsterdam. I stand on Voorburgstraat on a busy Friday night and the crowd swallows me up. Men of all sizes, shapes, colors surround me. I float along carried by a testosterone wave.

To my right is the canal, on my left, in buildings centuries old, in a string of windows glittering with light, a garden of earthly pleasures unfolds.

A few men stand in front of a window lit with Christmas lights watching a foxy older woman dressed like a gypsy, a flowered scarf wound round her head. She gathers the front of her full skirt up with one hand to reveal tattered black fishnet stockings held up by red garters that cut into her swarthy legs. With her other hand, she plunges a wine bottle in and out between her thighs. She leers, grimaces, sticks out her tongue. The men whistle and clap as I move on.

In the next window, a woman in a gray rubber cat suit stands with her back to the street. A big circle had been cut out of the seat of her pants, exposing her voluminous, pale ass. Her hands behind her, her fingers spread her butt cheeks, the swollen, ruby bud of her anus pulled open. She flexes her hips in rhythm to a song only she can hear, making her gaping asshole open and close.

"Do you think we can both fit in there, mate?" the man beside me asks his friend.

"Nah," says the friend. "My Churchill is so big. I'd crowd you out."

The first time I was in Amsterdam, in May 2001, America was a respected world power. I believed the prosperity we enjoyed would continue to grow. Now everything is different. My country is hated all over the world, our economy, bankrupt by war. At least, here in Amsterdam, Voorburgstraat appears unchanged, an enduring testament to fair-market exchange and the everlasting need of skin for skin.

On my last visit, I'd head for this street in the evenings. I'd walk up and down, turned on by the costumes, the artifice, the blatant aura of sex.

Then I met Jan and we were together until I left.

He was an overweight accountant I met in a bar. His hands were grimy, his fingernails stained with black ink, but his chubby, uncut cock was so practiced. He made me come again and again; then he'd pull out and shoot between my breasts. He liked to rub his creamy sperm all over my torso. It worked like a potion, erasing the memories of my ex-husband I still carried deep in my flesh.

One time, Jan took me to a dim courtyard guarded by a tarnished statue of Spinoza. The women in the windows here were all freaks. One was a glistening albino, totally hairless, not a blemish anywhere on her skin. She wore a cowboy hat on her bald head. Another woman looked like Larry King. She even wore thick eyeglasses with dark frames. She had on men's trousers but was nude from the waist up, three pretty breasts spreading across her broad chest. Jan paused before a window in which a serene, exotic beauty sat on a footstool. She looked Indonesian, her long black hair falling to her waist. One of her arms stopped at the elbow and the left sleeve of her gauzy shirt was pinned up at the shoulder. "This is Purple Tulip," he said, "She is an old friend of mine, very nice person, so gentle. Shall we visit her?"

I could see her pendulous breasts through her top; her tiny nipples looked like licorice bits.

"No," I whispered.

Jan shrugged, "Let's go back to your hotel," he said.

A few months ago, I was invited to Amsterdam to read at a poetry festival. I phoned Jan right up. He was delighted. "Good" he said, "My wife and mistress are away. You want to stay here?"

I didn't know how I would feel when I saw him. "Nah," I said, "your harem could come back and surprise us."

"Then we'll have an orgy," he said.

"We would give you a heart attack. Forget it. I'm staying in a hotel. I'll meet you when the festival is over."

During our affair, I felt I could trust him. He was fair-minded, sensitive, never tried to get over on me. If I shivered, he would take off his jacket and put it around my shoulders before I could even say a word.

As I walk along, I wonder if he is still friends with Purple Tulip. I wonder if I could find the courtyard of freaks without him.

Deep in my thoughts, I don't realize that I'm surrounded. Several young punks, not much more than boys, are gathered in a circle around me. Their heads are shaved and they wear wife-beater T-shirts. One of them also wears a pair of pantyhose looped around his neck like a tie. On his arm he has a tattoo of a pig, with MAMA inscribed beneath it.

"Looking for your husband?" he asks me. "Do you think he is shopping here?" His crew starts to laugh.

"Come with us," he continues. "We can help you find him." He looms over me, smelling of pizza and cigarettes. He reaches toward me. A phalanx of beefy British men in green-and-white rugby shirts cut into our little circle. I dart back out into the crowd.

"Good luck," pig boy calls after me. I hear them cackling but they don't follow me. I keep going until I find the dark alley that leads to Warmoesstraat.

Back in my hotel room, I get the hash pipe and my stash of Lebanese Red out of the night table drawer. I pull the covers over my head, hoping for sweet dreams.

Jan stands above me, naked. His huge belly hangs in folds like the Buddha's. His long cock is twice the size I remember, jutting out between his legs like another limb. He spanks me with it, little taps on my belly, my breasts. Each smack sends a current of electricity down into my hole. I want Jan to stop spanking me. I want him to plunge that thing right up into the center of my being, but he doesn't.

He teases and taps until I am writhing about like the Madwoman of Chaillot. Then, abruptly, he stops and steps back as Purple Tulip enters the room. Her face is lovely. All she wears is a garland of purple flowers wound round the stump of her arm. She kneels by the bed, extends her one delicate hand. Her fingers track though the forest of my pubic hair, dip into the syrupy well she finds there. I want to have her fuck me with her delicate fingers. I spread my legs as wide as I can but she draws her hand back. She slides the stump of her other arm up to the top of my thigh. I can feel it's warm, blunt tip inching into my cunt. All of a sudden, the room fills with men shouting, clapping their hands, and stamping their feet.

"Good luck, good luck," they shout, their taunting grows louder and louder into a tumultuous roar. I wake up and reach for the hash pipe I left on the bed table. I smoke until I black out.

The bells at the Alte Kirche down the street are ringing the hour. I jump out of bed. I'm supposed to meet my Jan today at ten. He is probably already waiting. My head feels stuffed with old socks, but I force myself to dress and run outside. I dash two blocks up Warmoesstraat and enter Dam Square.

Directly in front of me, at least three stories high, stands the white stone obelisk called the Dam. It's still so early, few tourists are about, but the demonstrators are already there.

A bearded man with a megaphone is leading them as they sing "Give Peace a Chance." They are holding placards in English, Dutch, French, German. Several of them show that photo of Lynndie England with the poor Iraqi man on a leash, no caption necessary. I wish I was wearing a T-shirt that said, "I am Canadian." I dart through the demonstrators quickly, my head down. I take the narrow street that cuts into the south end of the square. I pass a shop window filled with pipes, bongs, brass hookahs, and hookahs set with shining gems. Next to this store is Jan's favorite café.

A couple is eating croissants at the first table. Seated behind them at the second table is Jan, but a bigger Jan. He has gained so much weight; his chair is pushed back from the table to accommodate his bulging stomach. He rises, his belly knocking over the glass of water in front of him, but he is impervious. He steps forward, grabs me, kisses me smack on the lips. I feel like there is a giant marshmallow between us, but his mouth is dry and his lips as hot as I remember.

"I'm so happy to see you. You look beautiful, like movie star. Sit down," he says. I sit, and he sits beside me and takes my hand. His palms are moist and there are beads of sweat on his forehead.

"There's more of you," I say. "What happened, did you buy a candy store or become friends with a South American drug lord?"

"Do you think I am stupid?" he asks. "If you mean cocaine, that's a bad drug. I always avoid it. I developed a thyroid problem. It runs in my family. Now there is more of me to love. You want a chocolate, with whipped cream?" he asks.

"All right," I say.

"How was the festival? Did you get a big audience for your reading?" he wants to know. He listens as I talk. His hands are clean and he even had a manicure. He wears a fine gray silk shirt and, despite his bulk, looks quite distinguished, like a young Orson Wells. Our hot chocolates arrive piled with thick whipped cream. It tastes so sweet. I think of Jan shooting his rich come all over my breasts. He moves his leg against mine under the table, "I hope you still find me attractive. I hope this," he says, patting his stomach, "doesn't discourage you."

"No," I say, "I'll still think you're cute even if you get as big as an elephant."

"Good," he says, grinning. "Maybe later I will let you rub my trunk."

"Do you still see Purple Tulip? Are you still friends," I ask. "Does she still do the same job?"

"Yes to all three," Jan answers. "You see, our mothers know each other since high school. Maybe you are ready to visit her?"

"Maybe," I say in a whisper. Suddenly I feel embarrassed. I change the subject, mention the demonstrators in Dam Square. Jan's expression darkens.

"What do you expect when you go to war for oil, when you elect a liar for a president?" His voice rises. "Now he is a murderer, a war criminal. He should be assassinated."

"Whoa, whoa," I reply, "We didn't elect him. The Supreme Court gave him the election."

"Exactly," he cries, almost yelling now, "and you Americans sat around watching football. Why not rise up, demonstrate, stop paying taxes?" I knew how right he was but I didn't want to get into a fight with him. "I agree," I said, "but who could have anticipated what was happening? We were in shock."

"Fools," he says. He grabs the cup in front of him and drinks his chocolate down in one gulp, leaving specks of whipped cream around his mouth.

"I feel worse than you do, believe me," I say. "Let's try to keep our spirits up. Shall we smoke?" He doesn't answer, just sits there fuming.

Finally, he looks up, gives me half a smile. "Okay," he says, "we will change perspective." He calls the waiter to bring over the menu. "Will it be hashish or marijuana?" he asks. We decide on Blue Mountain Thai Stick. I roll a perfect oval joint.

Jan moves his chair closer to mine, lights the joint with the match from the pack on the table. He holds it first to my lips then to his. He puts one heavy hand on my knee. Blue smoke envelops us and then we are walking on a blue beach beside a blue ocean. Jan kneels in front of me, pulls my skirt up and my panties down. He cups my ass in his hands and pulls me closer. He parts my cunt hair with his blue tongue, traces a path to the top of my slit, finds my clit, which is already hard as a pearl. He sucks and sucks it; his hands cradle my ass as gentle blue waves wash about us. When I come, I cry blue tears.

I wipe the salty brine from my eyes and then I am back with Jan at our table. My hand is inside Jan's trousers, while his hand has found it's way beneath my skirt. The waiter and the man who tends the counter in the back are chatting quietly. A few tables away two priests share a hash pipe. Jan leans over, kisses me on the forehead.

"You want to come to my place tonight?" he asks.

"Oh, yes," I say.

I put on a short skirt so Jan can admire my legs and a scoop-neck blouse so he can see the tops of my breasts. I hear a slurred male voice right outside my door say, "She told me I was the best fuck she ever had, the best fuck in her whole life. She asked me, please, please, come back again tonight."

I walk up to Central Station and take the number eleven bus to Jan's flat in Java Plein.

I knock on Jan's door.

He opens it after a few minutes, naked except for a big white towel knotted around his waist. He is so heavy he looks ready to tip over. I tell myself to think positive. He is a nice man. I can trust him.

"Come in, come in," he says. "I just got back from my office late. I was in the shower. Pardon my formal attire." I follow him into his living room, a pleasant oasis filled with plants and antiques. "Sit down," he says. "I will bring drinks," then he goes into the kitchen.

I sit on the big maroon sofa and put my bag on the coffee table in front of me.

Jan returns, carrying a tray holding a bottle of wine, two glasses, a dish piled with black olives. He puts the tray on the coffee table.

"I remember you like Reisling," he says as he pours me a glass. "Now for music, some Brubeck?" he asks, but doesn't give me a chance to answer, just slips the disk into the CD player and goes back down the hall to his bedroom.

He returns wearing a pair of beige trousers and a white shirt big as a tent. He is holding a small foil-wrapped package in his hand.

"You look so lovely sitting there," he says, "like a little flower, a daisy." I didn't like being compared to a daisy, such a placid Pollyanna flower.

He sinks down beside me and puts the foil packet on the coffee table.

"Now," he says, "since we haven't seen each other in so long, a special celebration is in order. I got for us some of our famous Amsterdam space cake."

Jan unwraps the cake from the foil. "Here," he says, breaking off a piece and holding it to my lips, "have a taste."

It tastes like the honey cake my grandmother used to bake on Rosh Hashanah, sweet and mealy. We feed the cake to each other bit by bit, washing it down with wine. Jan puts his roly-poly arm along the back of the couch. I nest into his body, unbutton his shirt. A great, big cloud, all white and puffy, falls out. It grows, surrounding my face, my whole body, like a soft cushion. I float within this billowing white; Jan is there, too, his clothes gone. We are suspended in the cloud, floating together. Jan drifts below me. I reach out to him and my fingers fall on his swollen club. It grows larger and larger until it just pops out of my hand. I can feel the heat of it moving across my ass as it grows even hotter, like a desert wind, a sirocco. The pointy tip jabs into my crack. I pull away, my butt hole contracting, closing. The last time we tried this, Jan lubed me up with half a stick of margarine, and even though I was no stranger to back-door sex, I started to bleed. We had to stop.

Now Jan reaches up to my face. He has a capsule in his hand and he breaks it right under my nose.

"Breathe in, breathe deep," he says, and then his huge joint slides into me. I hear a tearing sound and feel a tingling sensation but no pain. As he moves deeper into my belly, Jan keeps murmuring something in my ear. I strain to hear him. "I fuck you in the ass, America," he whispers. Even in my spacey state, I can't believe what he is saying.

"What was that? What did you say?" I ask him. "Fuck you, America, fuck you America," he hisses, pumping harder and harder. Now I can feel him hurting me. I smell blood. I try to pull my body away but cannot move. I am skewered on a burning spit. His teeth are sharp on my neck and then he bites down, piercing my skin. I scream as he shoots bolts of fire into me. There are searing flames everywhere; every cell in my body is consumed and then it is dark.

When I open my eyes, my head is on Jan's leg. He is sleeping, snoring through his nose. My neck aches from where he bit me and my butt hole burns. I look down and see blood all over my thighs. I put my hand in my ass and bring it out covered with blood.

Carefully, I peel myself off him. I remember what Jan said and, briefly, wonder if I could have imagined it, but I know I did not. I'm so woozy I can barely stand, but I manage to totter to the bathroom. I shut the door and sit down on the toilet.

The seat feels comforting against my burning flesh. I want to find a washcloth, hold it against the bleeding to make it stop. I open a drawer in the cabinet beneath the sink and see a box of talcum powder and a bottle of mouthwash. I pull out the drawer next to it and find a sandwich bag filled with little chunks of what looks like rock candy. I have seen this "candy" before; it is crack cocaine. Beside it are some plastic bags of white powder. The drawer also holds a glass pipe, a rectangular mirror, a mat knife—all you need to enter a fool's paradise.

I slam the drawer shut. So much for trust. I open the drawer below and find the cloths I am looking for. I pick one up, hoping I can grab my clothes and get out while Jan is still sleeping. It is already too late. He steps into the bathroom, grinning like a Cheshire cat.

"So," he asks, "do you like our Dutch space cake—but, my little darling, what are you doing sitting on the toilet? Meditating?"

I nod my head, unable to speak. I spread my legs and lift my body so he can see the blood coming from my ass. He is instantly solicitous; he takes the cloth from my hand, opens another drawer, gets out Mercurochrome, Band-Aids.

"There," he says, after staunching the bleeding and cleaning and dressing the cut, "now you are fine." He pulls me to my feet. "I have something else for you, a surprise I know you will like." He starts pulling me down the hall toward his bedroom.

"Wait," I say, "I just remembered, I have to go back to my hotel. I have to call my father in Maryland. He's expecting my call, he's—"

Jan tightens his grip on my wrists. "You can call him from here," he says. He is stronger than and I am, an iron force, and he pulls me into the bedroom.

"You will like this, trust me, it will be fun," he says.

Purple Tulip is lying on the paisley quilt that covers Jan's bed. She is naked except for the garland of purple flowers around the stump of her arm. She is reading a *Seventeen* magazine, which she puts down as we enter the room.

"Hello," she says and smiles. Close up she does not look beautiful. Her skin is pocked; her eyes are blank and yellow. She is missing a front tooth, and her smile is rigid, as if stitched on to her face.

Jan pushes me forward from the back, "What are you afraid of?" he says. "Go to her, go say hello."

I feel like I'm moving quicker than the speed of light as I whirl, duck under his arm, and rush back down the hall. He is startled, hesitates a second before he turns and starts to lumber after me. He catches his foot on the edge of the rug, trips, and falls to the floor, crashing in a big puddle of flesh.

I grab up my things as Jan calls out, "American cow! Coward!" but nothing he can say has the power to hurt me now. I fly out the door and down the stairs. I pause in the vestibule, pull on my clothes and shoes.

The night is clear and warm. At least I managed to escape with only a cut-up ass. Not another soul is about, but the smell of ganja hangs in the air, mixed with something else: the scent of an exotic spice, cardamom or coriander. The strains of klezmer music drift out an open window. There are no stars in the sky but there is plenty of light as I walk toward the bus stop under an Amsterdam full moon.

MILK

MICHELLE RICHMOND

How they come to her, one by one, in the forest of their cho-
sen exile. It is a time of drought of both the physical and spiritual
varieties—a lack of water and maternal love. She is a modern day
Rose-of-Sharon, proffering her swollen breasts to grown men in
need. Their tribe believes that soldiers who have drunk from the
breast of a white woman are invincible in battle. Their tribe op-
poses the encroachment of a foreign government on sacred land,
the destruction of trees, the plundering of rivers.

She can almost see their point—almost. But there are, she believes, greater things at stake: democracy, progress, the very rush
of modernity.

She is not of their tribe, but they have invited her in. They have a name for her that cannot be translated into English. There are twenty-eight fighters in this encampment. Often, soldiers visit from other camps. At night, in pairs, they come to her, naked except for an amulet they wear around their necks. They shave their heads before nursing, so that each man is bald as a babe.

Two years and two months ago she gave birth. Her own boy has long since been weaned, sent back to America to live with relatives. On orders from her government, she kept the milk flowing until she could infiltrate their tribe. She sleeps in a hut the soldiers have lovingly built for her, with a floor of matted straw. They feed her palm wine and coconuts and small animals they have killed and roasted. The meat tastes of fire and of the sticks on which it is skewered.

She loves the heft of her breasts before nursing, the way the milk fills her until the skin stretches tight. When she hears them treading the path to her hut over dead branches and fallen leaves, two at a time, her breasts tingle in anticipation, the nipples tighten, her shirt is soaked with warm milk.

What she did not expect, what has come as a complete surprise, is the bliss: theirs and hers. The way a grown man's eyes will look hungry and sometimes mean as he latches on, but will roll back in his head as he drinks his fill, infantile. The way she becomes damp and needy, opening her legs to allow their bare knees to press against her. She rocks back and forth against them while they nurse, glad for the fact that her government's technology doesn't reach here, into the heart of the forest. She is certain the men in their brightly lit offices would find her lust unbecoming, unnecessary, at odds with the spirit of her mission.

Sometimes the men suck themselves into a state of half-conscious ecstasy, the milk dribbling out of the corners of their mouths. Sometimes they ejaculate while drinking. Sometimes she does, too, dreaming of God and country, her own bright sacrifice.

Sometimes they bite down and their teeth leave marks. There is a certain one who always draws blood, every time. She thinks of him during the day while she lies alone in her hut, waiting. She would like to kiss him afterward, would like to taste her milk on his tongue, the sweet-sour tang of it.

Late at night, after nursing, they fuck her, two at a time: one with his cock, the other with his hand. She has never been fucked so beautifully and so desperately as these men fuck her, dreaming, perhaps, of their wives and mothers. She, meanwhile, thinks of her son back home with her family. By now he must be speaking in sentences, and learning the alphabet. She is proud that he will grow up in an omnipotent country, an empire uncompromised by the whims of smaller nations; she hopes that he will understand her own small contribution.

Unbeknownst to the guerillas, she has been ingesting a toxic chemical substance which, upon entering her body, concentrates itself in her milk. Each night, after the men have left her hut, she injects herself with an antidote. It will not keep her safe forever, but it will keep her alive long enough to complete her work. It is important work, her government assures her. Necessary work. Work only a woman can do.

A few of the soldiers have already begun to show signs of illness—the characteristic yellow eyes and swollen glands, the deteriorating joints. Believing it is some mosquito-borne disease, they treat it with useless medicines, dress the joints with pointless salves. And still they come to her, mouths agape with hunger and lust, blind to the traitor in their midst. Still they fuck her with a passion completely beyond any she has known before. Even the father of her son was temperate in comparison, filling her with his sperm casually, noncommittally, on the night they met. It happened at a party, in the bathroom. He shoved her against the wall; he did not take off his clothes.

So unlike these men, who trust her with their bare skin, their unfathomable hope. She is touched by their faith, awed by the power of their mythology: that they could invest someone like her, so ordinary in every way, with such power.

She is not alone. She does not know how many others like her are scattered among the hills and forests. Every one of them is an unwed mother. Every one of them has been persuaded that this is the way to make amends, to save her family's honor and make her country proud. She imagines that one day books will be written about her kind. There will be documentaries, posthumous praise. Medals of honor are not out of the question. Maybe some of the women will even survive to tell their stories. She knows she will not be one of them. Lately, her body has succumbed to strange pains; she feels sometimes as though a place is being hollowed out inside her, in the vicinity of her kidneys. She can almost feel something there, like a small and hungry animal gnawing away.

She has a secret hope: that one day her son will visit this country, retrace the steps of the soldiers, and find the place where she is buried, her place among the men.

SOCIAL CONTRACT

STEPHEN ELLIOTT

"You have the right to bear arms," she says, slipping the ropes through my fingers, and then around my elbows, pinning them painfully together and cinching them through the window handle above my head. "Just not these arms."

Her skin is the color of pasta. She has large cheeks, a careful mouth. "Harry Truman invented the national security state," she says, my right leg pulled at the ankle by a long cord that finally connects at the base of a radiator. My other leg is spread, the rope looped around the refrigerator. My legs are akimbo, my body utterly vulnerable. "The people have to be afraid, Truman said. That was the way Harry Truman thought. We have to fear the communists. Franklin Roosevelt was dead. Long live Franklin Roosevelt."

The nipple clamps hurt. The ball gag she has stuffed into my mouth makes it impossible for me to answer her, if there was an answer to be given. She didn't ask me if I wanted this. She's stronger than me, especially since my accident. I never fight her anymore. She does what she wants.

"The Geneva Convention holds that you can't torture prisoners. America is a signatory to the Geneva Convention. Are you a prisoner?" I nod my head. She closes my nose shut with two fingers. I can't breathe through the gag she has forced into my mouth. There is a moment of peace. This is it, I think. I am going to die. And then my body starts to flop, the panic coming through me involuntarily, and she's laughing, and she lets go of my nose, and the air rushes into my body in deep, sweeping breaths, and her laughter fills the room with its cruelty.

"We don't care about treaties," she says. "Hitler didn't care about Versailles and they gave him Czechoslovakia, the Rhineland, and Austria. Anschluss. That's what they call it. But Hitler had his problems. Repressed homosexual." Her hand runs along my stomach and the top of my leg and then down beneath me, her finger touching my anus. "Are you a repressed homosexual? You don't seem to like sex very much. I think you are." I feel her finger slip slightly into my anus and then out. "So he died in a bombed-out bunker in Berlin in 1945, with his new wife. What the hell for?" I watch as she stands and walks to the closet and dips through the door, rummaging through the sound of paper bags. She has such long legs. She's a cyclist. Her long thin body is knotty with strips of muscles. Then she's in front of me, between my legs, looking gleefully into my eyes, forcing something large into my ass. I scream into the gag, a muffled gasp, a blunt, dulled shriek. Whatever it is goes in and it burns and it stays there, throbbing slowly. The pain begins to subside. But she still has something in her hand and she squeezes it and an electric shock shoots through my bowels, my eyes bulging in my face, my body pouring sweat onto the sheets.

"I was wondering if that would work."

She smiles, warmly, happy and content. It's been twelve years now since the first day we met. A couple of waiters in a young restaurant on the edge of the city, working to make ends meet. We didn't know what we had.

"We don't care about treaties," she continues. "In 1954 Eisenhower signed a treaty that provided for free elections in Vietnam in two years' time. But when it came due he changed his mind. He said if Vietnam had free elections, Ho Chi Minh would receive eighty percent of the vote. And that wouldn't be good for America. So much for democracy. Do you feel cheated? Look at the Iranians. The Shah served us well for twenty-five years. Then they took hostages." She steps forward, her naked foot on my stomach. She walks over me and then places her foot on my face. She rubs her foot over my face, back and forth, across my nose. She steps on the clamp on my nipple, and I let out another involuntary dull scream. "Cheated by our vows to have and to hold, to love and to cherish, to protect, till death do us part. Do you think we've parted too early? Did you think things would be different when you pledged your allegiance in school, and at the baseball games? That your country would protect you while the bombs fell and U.S.-installed dictators sent death squads into the villages of South and Central America to kill the women and children first? Here is your democracy." Her foot presses hard on my face, and my nose hurts. I think it's going to break. With the heel of her foot she pushes the gag farther toward the back of my throat. Tears spring from my eyes, soaking the fabric around my ears. "You should be able to answer some of my questions. You should.

"I'm not blaming America," she says, sitting heavily on my chest and then turning around, facing away from me. Her long back, straight and proud, the bulb of spine and her dark hair which she's taken to wearing short. She's wrapped a chain around my penis and balls and she's slowly making it tighter. "I was born here, same as you. I'm not blaming anybody. It's just that you have the right to remain silent, and maybe the Republicans really did win the election, and maybe they didn't. It's too close to call. Both sides believed in three strikes, you're out. Life sentence, no parole. How many strikes do you have?" she asks, turning her head to me briefly and then going back to her task. "There's no welfare here. You'll have to work for what you get."

I've surrendered myself to the continuous pain. I've allowed the pain running through my body to numb my mind. This is my wife. This is what we have. Who would have thought we would have lived in this apartment all this time.

"And then the wars came." Another shock rings through the electric plug in my ass, pain striking through me, her hand in my hair pulling hard, her other along my ribs, buckling forward as if she were riding a horse, her feet sliding back toward my cheeks. And then stopping. She's loosening the chains. Gently wrapping her thumb and forefinger around my penis and balls. "And they flew planes into our buildings and our buildings crumpled and fell to the ground. We have to defend ourselves. They would have done it anyway, whether we deserved it or not. That's the way people are. And the president didn't want to consult Congress anymore. He asked them to dissolve themselves, to remove themselves from the conflict. And of course they did. Self-preservation in the face of terror.

She slides her body back, so her ass is just in front of my nose, the smell of her and her flesh totaling my vision.

"Do you remember Bukharin?" she asks. "It was 1936, and he confessed in a public address to the people. He turned on his fellow Bolsheviks, Kamenev, Trotsky, Zinoviev, all Jews. He wanted to save himself. But Stalin placed him under house arrest anyway. *Koba, why do you need me to die?* he asked in his unanswered letter to Stalin. But who was he to ask for forgiveness? All of the original Bolsheviks subscribed to a doctrine of terror, of starving their own people. It was merely the rooster coming home to roost." Her hand is in my mouth, fishing out the gag, plucking it from between my cheeks. She rubs her fingers inside my lips, massaging my gums. And she's right, I breathe so much easier now. She undoes the rope at my ankles, and my knees slide together, my legs bending on their own will. She undoes my hands from the window and releases my elbows but keeps my hands tied together. My hands tied, I curl into a ball, pulling the tear-soaked sheet with me. And she curls behind me, her body circling my body, her knees forcing between my knees, one hand underneath my head and across my chest, the other between my legs, gripping my penis. I can feel her body, her strength which seems to increase every day even as mine declines. Her body is so firm, intent, and purposeful.

"My darling," she says, a whisper, her voice like the cars on the street, penetrating into the darkness. Thank God for the evenings, when the sun is down. "I'll protect you." Her breath swimming across my ear, searching through my hair. "You don't have to worry. Never worry. Never ever worry again. I am here. I will keep you safe."

WARGY AND ENERGY POLICY

KEITH KNIGHT

209

DIRTY HEAVEN

VANESSA NORTON

When I was twenty-four I got an entry-level job with a left-of-center political party canvassing neighborhoods I'd only pondered while riding the subway. Sheepshead Bay, Ozone Park, Maspeth, Middle Village, Utopia, tiny, round pills paused along the B, Q, M, and C lines. These places could have been in another country, they seemed that remote, that exotic.

Our crew varied from five to fifteen, each of us part of a campaign to raise the minimum wage. Mondays through Thursdays the canvassing manager, a retired cop named Bernie, propelled us down thoroughfares of car dealerships lit by blurry brake lights, marooned us on residential corners far from rush-hour traffic, fast food chains, the random independent grocer. We emerged from the van carrying clipboards, stacks of party literature, envelopes for funds collected. Our nightly goal was thirty signatures and a hundred bucks. The first night I amassed eighty-six dollars, minus the beer I nursed at a local bar.

The following nights proved even less lucrative for the organization; I pilfered all small bills and quarters. Even when the lit faces of attached houses seemed to be the only ones looking, I slid the money under my palm, along the yoke of my jeans, and into my back pocket. Later, I rewarded myself with drink or a trip down Duane Reade's candy aisle.

A few weeks into the campaign, an elderly lady answered her door in a quilted pink robe buttoned to the neck. She was a fragile woman with yellow-brown skin powdered a sallow golden hue. I lamented my cause with an orphan's dignity. *How can anyone survive on five dollars and twenty-five cents an hour? Look at me,* I nearly said, holding out my cold hands.

Just when I thought she might retreat, another old lady approached the door. This time a fat one in a blue robe. Morning glories twisted up her front, around her collar. Immediately, I wanted in. I wanted to sit in their living room, between them and listen to them giggle. I stopped talking—and before I knew it, they had held the door open and were ushering me to a beige velveteen sofa patterned in feathery paisleys, cockatiels flying between them. The small woman stepped into the kitchen, reappeared with a Styrofoam cup of coffee, clumps of sweetened, congealed oil floating on its surface.

"She doesn't like to do dishes," the fat one said. Her cheeks reminded me of the flat, baggy rump of a pachyderm.

"Neither do you!" the smaller one giggled.

Their English was heavily accented. Between talking to me,

they mumbled indecipherable colloquialisms. I nearly nodded off just looking at them, their loveliness had that effect. I asked to use their bathroom, ferried through their murmuring.

The bathroom was pink as the inside of a conch. Above the toilet was a brass shelf with three mirrored shelves, the top of which displayed a smudged silver compact. I took it off the shelf and examined its exterior. Tiny blossoms rose from its silver, gathered into wreaths below its clasps. Inside, it was empty— no mirrors, no powder. But for a moment, the compact rested in my palm like someone's heart. I closed my eyes, dragged my fingertip over petals and pistils and leaves tiny as a newborn's fingernail. I wanted it to be mine forever. And easily it could have. At home, my dresser was a gallery of stolen ornaments, from an antique sapphire ring to a Mont Blanc fountain pen to a knife engraved with the initials *FOG*—and nothing, really, but my own conscience, which my life up until now had confirmed to be a parched gully, kept me from stealing it. Nothing. But in that moment, I discovered something I'd always doubted: I couldn't. I didn't have it in me.

I waited for Bernie at the intersection of Queens Blvd and Forty-ninth. Across the meridian, SUVs roared past a pizza joint announcing itself in blinking green neon. Inside, my restraint was blossoming into pride. I had to jog in place just to keep up with its momentum. *You're good*, it told me. *Good.* When the minivan approached, Bernie lowered his window and a feather of sleet landed on his wide, white mustache.

He asked:"Too much coffee?"

"No. I'm just keeping warm." The fact was, I'd removed my woolen hat and gloves, I was burning up.

"How'd we do?" His lips stretched into the kind of smile you give when you know someone has gotten lucky.

"I only got thirty—" I said, "Thirty-two," remembering the two dollars in my back pocket.

I sat in front with Bernie. There were four others in back, but during the ride to downtown Brooklyn, they didn't exist. Not that I'd ever talked much to anyone, but now they seemed to have vaporized, re-frozen as feathery patterns on the back windshield. I told Bernie about the two ladies. I told him about the coffee in the Styrofoam cup, and the cockatiels flying through the upholstery of their couch. I wanted to tell him everything—about the compact and my moment of divine intervention, but to do so would have meant incriminating myself for all my wrongdoings of the past. So I ended right there. Bernie nodded and grunted in agreement—he appreciated little old ladies, too—without asking how long I'd stayed or if they had donated any money. (They hadn't.)

"You know we're moving to Manhattan," he said. The tips of his mustache bristled against his blue nylon coat.

"No."

"We just endorsed a Democrat for state senate and we've been hired to vote-canvass her district. I think you should help run the office up there."

"Me?"

"Why not? You've been around longer than most, and I think you're smart. Besides, you know how easy this shit is."

I shrugged my shoulders, realizing this wasn't as flattering as I'd hoped.

Bernie hadn't left Brooklyn his entire life and he wasn't going to start now. So, four days a week, I rode my bike up the path along the West Side Highway to Seventy-ninth Street, risking my life through traffic to arrive early at our office, a hovel on the ground floor of a featureless, rent-subsidized high-rise. The voting district consisted of a hefty chunk of Manhattan stretching from Fourteenth Street into the nineties. My job was piling the voters' addresses into stacks, assigning each stack to a clipboard, then pairing up staff. As someone accustomed to reducing most of my shift to a break, I thought the right kind of pairing might discourage this. My staff was a convenient miscellany of do-gooders and derelicts, including a dull-eyed environmentalist with the complacency of a Mormon and a magenta-haired foster kid with whom I'd once spent an entire shift in Maspeth, passing a liter of Heineken.

But those days were over. I stuck the foster kid with the environmentalist, entrusting one to foil the other. I felt like a hypocrite but imagined most people felt this way.

Every evening, I picked someone to accompany me through my list of apartment buildings, ride the elevator to the top floor, knock our way to the basement, zigzagging down stairwells, sliding campaign fliers under security doors, cutting off the squinting eyes and thinning hair and sloping forehead of our candidate's face. Once my staff understood the routine was for real, no one wanted to accompany me. Most days we were an oddly numbered crew; I canvassed alone.

Then, in late June—just in time for the hot, humid weather to set in, just in time to trade in my jeans and long-sleeved T-shirt for an Indian cotton skirt and a tank top, and just in time to ditch my bra—a new guy showed up.

"He's all yours," Bernie told me over the phone. "Show him the ropes."

The guy appeared to be about my age; skinny, with a plump adolescent mouth and tortoiseshell glasses. His boyish form carried an airy, weightless quality; he seemed to be floating under the open doorway, shifting in and out of the frame, blurred by the outside light.

"I'm Russell," he said, stepping inside. He was dressed in an ugly red-and blue-striped shirt with a white V-neck collar out of which a cluster of reddish hairs sprouted. He moved with calculated indifference, but tagging it as such gave me a fragile impression of knowing him.

I surrendered my stack of lit to him, tucked the clipboard and canvassing sheets under my arm. As we ambled up Lexington, I asked for his impressions of our candidate.

"Didn't she put in like ten years at a homeless shelter?"

He turned to face me as he spoke, while I remained with my nose to the sidewalk.

"That happens to be the first thing I remember about her," I said.

As we continued up the street, I undressed every bar and deli we passed, stripping them of fiberglass and paint and concrete, until they were nothing but a neat row of bottles, a saucer of smoked fish, a bowl of ice cream. I had to remind myself that I cared about my job now because I was the boss, that I was trying to pay attention these days. I hadn't stolen anything from work. I'd minimized my breaks. I wanted people to trust me. I wanted to be good.

Our first apartment building was yellow bricked with a dark green awning. Barrels of geraniums fortified either side of the front walk. Russell and I stood at the switchboard of buzzers as if we knew someone in the building, until a man in a starchy white shirt exited and Russell grabbed the door. In the elevator, we divided the sheets according to floor—he took the ones on top, and I took the rest. When I handed him a pen, we brushed thumbs and locked eyes, and briefly I felt something surreptitious pass between us.

"I'll meet you outside in thirty minutes," I said.

He nodded, then the doors closed.

I went from apartment to apartment, hoping the person wouldn't be home so I could ponder my attraction to Russell, strategize the rest of our evening.

It was only 6:35 when we met outside. Russell was sitting on the edge of a barrel of geraniums smoking.

"Hey," he said. His voice was soft and hauntingly familiar; it seemed as though we'd been friends early in life, as preschoolers, the ones who'd slunk away from the group to hide in tall grasses, emerging with one hand down the front of their pants.

"It's early," I said, glimpsing a kissing couple across the street.

He pulled a throatful of smoke.

"We could get a drink," I said, then added, "It helps to be relaxed when you talk to strangers."

We found a surprisingly dank place—or maybe it seemed that way because it was so bright outside. The only light bled from a row of golden bulbs reflected off the varnished wood of the bar top. We set our campaign materials down and ordered pints of Guinness.

"I feel like we've fallen into our own dirty heaven," I said, swallowing one, then two gulps.

"Me, too," he said.

"I was really—so—in the mood for this."

"Exactly in the mood," he said.

I wanted to kiss him, but it was better to stew in flirtation for as long as possible. He brushed my bare shin with his. I sipped the remaining foam from my glass and ordered another round. As we drank, Russell disclosed the obvious facts about his life: he was twenty-three—a year younger than me—and from Rhode Island. He hadn't finished college because he'd gone on the road with a band his junior year and never went back. Now his life was dedicated to music.

"I used to live with a musician. I wouldn't repeat the experience."

"We don't make good partners," he said.

"It wasn't that," I said, even though it was.

We drank some more. A thirtysomething man in chinos sat at the other end of the bar smoking. I slid off my stool and walked over to him.

"Could you spare a cigarette or two?" I asked.

He looked at me with a strained expression but didn't say anything, then lifted two cigarettes from his chest pocket and held them out to me with a limp hand.

Russell talked about touring as we smoked and drank. I resisted telling him everything I knew about that kind of life, which was actually a lot, and something I felt I'd left behind a year before.

"I sort of got stuck in New Orleans," he said, twisting his face and scratching the back of his neck.

"You fell in love?"

"With dope."

"Oh, that," I said. "That's the one thing I didn't try in college. Practically everything else, but not that."

He didn't say anything. A tendril of his personality—the one that had lain his weakness on the bar for me to touch, the one I liked—seemed to curl up and disappear.

"I've always been curious." I drew on my cigarette. "You kicked it or what?"

"I keep it under control."

"You seem fine," I said. I thought of the junkies I'd known, peripherally, in college and wondered how often they were high without my realization. I remembered a guy who'd lived in the same house as a girl I spent weekends with. He was a twig of a man, with long, straight, wheat-colored hair and a face like a scarecrow's. We used to have short conversations while waiting to get into the bathroom. I couldn't remember any of them now. What I did remember was seeing the girl at a party months after we'd stopped talking, and her telling me he was dead.

Russell shrugged his shoulders and threw back his beer with a vigor that appeared almost healthy.

"When's the last time you did it?"

"Before I left for work." He smiled.

"Today?"

"Just a little," he said.

I hid my reaction—I didn't even know what *it* was—by drinking the last of my beer.

"We should get going." I slid off my barstool. It was light outside. I didn't want to be in the dark, but as soon as we were on the street, I regretted not kissing him inside.

The closest apartment building on our list was a block north on Eighty-ninth. We swaggered uptown with the buoyant flair of intoxication. We found the building and sneaked in under the guise of holding the door for an elderly woman in a beige house-dress who happened to be using a cane. "You're so kind," she told us, steadying the rubber tip of her cane with each tiny step. "Thank you, that's good." I turned to watch her drag herself to-ward the sidewalk.

"It always makes me sad to see someone struggling like that," I said.

"She was a sweet lady and she let us inside."

"Without suspicion."

Russell spotted the elevator without the least bit of delibera-tion. He pushed the twelfth-story button before I told him where we were going. This minor decision seemed to express an underly-ing willingness to take charge. We were still swayed by Guinness, and Russell had already told me too much. Nothing could ever be as it was intended when he'd walked into my office.

I extended my finger, touching the placket of his ugly shirt. Two transparent buttons had broken off; one hung from a strand of white thread. I nudged it with my nail until it balanced on my fingertip like a drop of water.

"What happened with this one?" I asked.

"I don't remember."

"There's no story?"

"If there were, you wouldn't want to know it."

"You're wrong."

The elevator released itself and lifted us toward the sky. He lowered his head onto my shoulder, rubbed his nose over my collarbone. Our mouths found one another and opened. We broke through our hesitations and celebrated in slurred grunts until the elevator held still and opened its door. We gasped, stepped into a long, cream-papered corridor with sconces of light glowing like scallop shells. Across the vestibule, a uselessly small inlet was carved into the wall. It seemed like the place for an end table and a lamp, but none was there. Russell grabbed my hand, dragged me to the inlet, where our lips reattached and our fingers groped beneath our clothes.

Then a door down the hall opened and shut. I heard the *swish-swish-swish* of approaching legs, but I didn't stop. His mouth was pouring into me.

When I turned my face, I caught the angular figure of a young woman sheathed in pink linen tapping the sole of her high heel against the carpeted floor. She sighed loudly. Our clipboard and lists of names and campaign pamphlets were scattered about our feet like waste. I lowered myself slowly, carefully grabbing the clipboard, as if subtle movements might save us from detection.

"What are you doing in this building?" The woman asked.

"We were just campaigning," I said, hoping she was at least a Democrat.

"Who let you in here? You're not allowed to be in here. If you don't get the hell out, I'm calling the police."

A metal exit door was next to the elevator. I hadn't noticed it before, but sure enough it was there. We rushed past the woman and into the stairwell, which had been painted vanilla and lit by fluorescent strips beaming from the ceiling. I quickly descended the stairs and Russell followed. For a brief moment, I thought I'd trip, my legs were moving so fast. Russell ran one floor below me, as if he were ready to ward off dragons or a janitor who wanted us out. Once I arrived on the second floor, I lost my will to continue. Sweat had beaded at my hairline. I waited on a landing, my back against the cool cinder-block wall, my arms at my sides, catching my breath. Russell stopped when he no longer heard my steps, then rushed up one flight of stairs and stood before me, his heart rising out of his chest.

"We don't have to leave here." His hands were on my face.

"I'm trying to be good."

"You're not trying very hard."

"I know." I plunged my tongue to the back of his mouth.

The rhythmic smack of someone's jeans against the inside of a dryer caught my attention. I took Russell's hand and lured him gingerly toward the basement. The final flight of stairs turned into a hallway smelling of mildew and the floral perfume of fabric softener. At the far end, a wall of windows cast misshapen blocks of light onto the cement floor.

"I want to find someplace to shoot up," Russell said.

"How long does it take?"

"A few seconds."

We entered a laundry room with walls painted the color of storm clouds. Dryers lined one side, washers the other, all shiny and white. I felt the urge to climb on top and sprint across the entire row. I abandoned my clipboard on the brown folding table, boosted myself onto a washing machine.

"I could do it in here," he said.

No one was around, but someone would be back. The dryer was running. Russell sprinted across the room and read the dial.

"Thirty minutes left."

"What if whoever comes early?"

"They won't."

He bowed slightly, kissed me, then reached into his pants pocket and retrieved a black eyeglass case. He crouched against the last dryer, facing the wall. I hid my hands behind my back, watched him pour yellowish powder from a square plastic bag into a spoon. He held a lighter beneath the spoon and the stuff bubbled into liquid. He pulled it into a tiny syringe; it was so small and clean and perfect the sight of it reminded me of how blameless we all begin. He hiked up his sleeve and shot it into a vein in the crook of his right arm, which was hardly scarred at all. I stared, knowing I was breaking some rule, but by then I felt he owed me something and all I wanted was to look at him.

Russell shook his head like a wet dog, then moaned.

"How do you feel?"

"Great," he said, tapping his fingers against the floor. "Thanks."

"For what?"

"I don't know. For being okay with this."

I offered my hand as if to pull him up, but he rose directly into my arms, wanting to be there, and for a moment I had him, all mine. His chest was sunken and the skin over his heart, thin; each pump of blood tapped like a finger on my breast. I wanted to hold it in my hands, just for a little while.

"I want to do some, too," I whispered.

"Are you sure?"

"Yes," I said, still in a hushed voice. "I know you have to ask, but I really do. Just once."

I half-expected to hear that there was no such thing as "once," but he said, "I have another needle."

"But just a little," I said, "I only want to taste it."

He dumped the remainder of the powder into the spoon and heated it with the lighter. It didn't look like much, but what did I know?

"Promise me it's not a lot," I said. "I don't want to be found in a laundry room."

"We're among clean things. Can't you be happy for this?"

"I am happy. Can't you tell?"

"All right," he said. "Let me see your veins."

I straightened my arm and turned it underside up. He ran his fingers along its center, pressing lightly on my most prominent vein. What a tender feeling, his fingertips playing against this protected piece of my body. His bewildered expression lifted into sudden piousness.

"Maybe you shouldn't look," he said.

"Just do it perfectly and only the littlest bit."

"I promise."

"Don't give me a bruise."

"I'll do my best."

"The best you've ever done."

"The best I've ever done."

I turned my head and squeezed my eyes shut. I winced when I felt the skin break, then drew a succession of deep breaths as the needle entered the center of my vein, him slowly pushing the plunger of the syringe, then pulling it out quickly.

He cradled my fingers into a limp fist, placing his entire hand over them like a birdcage. "If you're not dead now, you're fine," he said.

Before I could think to tell him that I felt nothing at all, the ceiling multiplied, drifting up and up and over and over and over again. Russell's eyes through his glasses were two gems of light, white-green tunneling backward. Unable to stand, I lay like a strip of rubber against the dryer, opened my mouth, released the continuous moan of a mean cat, then puked a small, gray puddle next to my hand. I examined its perfectly circular shape, wreathed in tiny rosebuds of saliva.

Russell wiped my mouth with the hem of his shirt. "At least it didn't land on your hand," he said. "That's what happened to me the first time."

I didn't answer—speaking now lay far beyond my capacity. I allowed my eyelids to drop and held myself in simple darkness, wondering where my clipboard was. I thought I heard Russell from down the hall, telling me something about the jeans, the jeans, almost dry, the jeans. Someone was coming. His fingers pet the hairs on my knee, brought my fist to my shoulder, closing my arm as if it were the hinge of a door, and at any moment we'd be lifted away.

CAPITOL
PUNISHMENT

LIZ HENRY

"The people! United! Shall never! Be! De-Feat-ed!"

"I fucking hate that chant," Jenna said. "It's so fucking stu-pid."

"Whatever. Just get on your knees and kiss me. Here," I said, grabbing the crotch of my leather pants. I smirked. She got on her knees and started licking my pants. Mosh, next to her, didn't need to be told. I yanked on her dog collar a little, and down she went to devote herself to my battered combat boots.

On the march we had been herded from the campus to the Capitol by anxious, strident rally officials. You could tell them from their orange safety vests. "Stay on the sidewalk!" they admonished through their megaphones. "Stay on the sidewalk! Walk in an Orderly Manner!" Cops on horses followed the snaking lines of the sidewalk march, ready to arrest anyone who didn't follow rally protocol.

Now, here, inside, the chants were amplified with strange echoes. We were in the very center of the star in the center of the room under the dome of the Texas Capitol. "NO MORE WAR! NO MORE WAR!" Good and rhythmic. I rocked my hips slightly to push my clit into Jenna's face. On her knees, she still had to bend over to reach; standing up, she was strong, tall, goddess-like, with a James Dean sneer. Jenna's black T-shirt—we'd made hundreds of them and still had boxes and boxes left to sell—said, "VISUALIZE BURNING POLICE CARS," in stark white letters. Even on her knees to me, Jenna still pissed me off. She wasn't submissive in every line of her body, like Mosh was. There was no sweetness. Jenna was all about a "whatever" brand of defiance. I felt even more defiance rise up in me and run right down hot into my cunt.

I looked around the room at the oil portraits of governors, the bronze plaques explaining history, the flags. I felt that I was at the heart of political power, and that heart was empty. Real power was somewhere else. Where? What was powerful? I was power, getting my boots and cunt licked by the fiercest activists in Austin. The rotunda of governors watched us benevolently as I grabbed Jenna's stiff-gelled mohawk and mashed into her face harder as if she were some sort of perverted merry-go-round horse made specially for me to masturbate on. Was anyone going to notice us? Could we get arrested for this? A few people had walked through—even a guard, and a woman in a power suit. The muffled echoing approach and fade of clicky heeled shoes. I looked up overhead the way I'd look at the moon if it were nighttime. The dome was glorious, huge, intricate. It could be a cathedral and we, a sleazy, dykey trio fucking right on the altar, on the Lone Star itself, deep in the heart of Texas. It was beautiful.

"Come on," I said. "Enough of this. Let's find the bathroom."

The chanting followed us through the hallways as we followed the signs. My cunt was wet and slippery next to the rough seams inside my pants. Mosh looked scared and trustful, like a little kid. "I can't believe you just DID that," she said in a whispery way. Her eyes were huge. For a supposedly tough butch dyke, when she went under, she really went under. She was regressing weirdly. "What if someone beat us up. Or something."

"Whatever. They're all too busy watching the circus outside."

"Shouldn't we be out there? I mean, the protest . . ." Mosh said guiltily.

Jenna snorted. "What, does it make you feel bad? Shouldn't you be out there right now? Is that going to do any good? You think Mommy Honorary Lesbian Anne Richards is going to listen to us? You think she can beat the oil boys? She couldn't even win against the biggest hick loser governor this state will ever see. Clayton fucking Williams! Ha! Fuck! Protest! Fucking fat lot of good it's going to do. We should be blowing shit up. Protest."

"I know, but maybe it will . . . and the media's covering it . . . and I'm missing CLASS . . ." She was getting whiny now. Soon she'd start blaming me for something and try to pick a fight. It was definitely time to fuck her. Preemptive fucking was the best strategy to make her shut up about money or her exams or how I loved Jenna best or how I wasn't a good enough top or how we'd left her out of the scene. "Maybe we should go back OUT there.

It's important to have a queer presence for the media . . . so that the world knows we're against the war . . ."

Jenna and I looked slyly at each other. She could read my mind on this point. I knew that, to her, we were both whiny, spoiled, middle-class bitches who bought our clothes at Contempo and Macy's instead of finding them in Dumpsters in back of the Army Surplus store like she did. All I asked was that she should channel her class hatred of me into really fucking hot sex.

"As IF it's going to make a difference," I hissed, slamming Mosh up against the wall of the handicapped stall. "Fucking idiot. Little hypocrite. You don't care if there's a war; you're at this stupid protest because I'm here. All you can do is stare at how my tits are hanging out." Jenna got behind her and grabbed her arms. We all wrestled for a minute, breathless. I yanked down Mosh's pants and started spanking her as hard as I could. No warmup.

"Ow! Sir! Ow! Ow What Did I Do, Sir?" she yelped.

"What did you do? Fucked around! Fucked around protesting for PETA and going to class like a good little girly-girl! Shit!"

"Ow! I'm sorry! I'm sorry! I'll do better next time! Oh please!"

Jenna started laughing and chimed in. "I bet you didn't even vote. Did you vote? Did you vote for Ann Richards?"

There was no answer. Just distant chanting.

"Voting is fucking stupid anyway," Jenna said. She spanked harder, in rhythm. The little metal anarchy buttons and air force pins on her jacket were clanking against each other. Mosh held on for dear life to the metal grab-bar. I held Mosh's face with one hand, nipped her little wire-rimmed glasses into my vest pocket, and carefully slapped her. Not like I'd hit Jenna. If we'd been alone I'd have choked her and punched her.

"I'm sorry! And I have a car! I'm part of the problem! I should ride my bike more!" Mosh whined as Jenna and I both slapped her around the bathroom stall. Her pants were down around her ankles and her ass was deep pink with slap marks. "Guys! We have to stop. We're going to get arrested! What if there's security cameras! This could ruin my career!"

Maybe she was right. But I didn't care. I wanted to get arrested. I didn't want us to be so safe. There was a war! I wanted to destroy something, to smash something, to light shit on fire. The police were pigs. The protesters were rainbow coalition hippies who signed petitions, stayed on the sidewalk, and didn't see any difference between fighting for peace and fighting for hemp. They hated us for discrediting their movement.

"I don't care if they arrest us. We might as well do something worth getting arrested for."

"Nobody's going to arrest us. God. You are both such dumb-asses," Jenna said, panting with effort as she held Mosh's wrists. "If you want to get arrested so bad, and you must, since you're always fucking talking about it, go punch a cop in the face." I couldn't tell if she was serious. She said once that she loved me. Sometimes I believed her.

"No. Seriously. Let's get out of here."

"Fuck that and fuck the war and FUCK YOU!" I slammed her up against the stall door, with my shoulder smashing against her strapped-down tits. I unzipped my vest pocket and got out a glove. It was getting to the point finally where latex smelled like sex to me instead of hospitals. "Fuck staying on the sidewalk." Mosh was wet and hot and whimpering. She was almost fainting with lust. Jenna held her up, crouched, spooning around Mosh's body, with NO BLOOD FOR OIL, NO BLOOD FOR OIL, helicopter thuds echoing through the granite halls and the tiled bathroom walls and the marble partitions between the bathroom stalls and the slick walls of Mosh's cunt warm and throbbing as I worked my fist in there and slammed her over and over again up against Jenna's soft body and bitterly thought of how real and live and warm our bodies were here safe in the Capitol Building and how we might die someday for something we believed in but not now because real death and oppression were far away from us three and our campus and our city. I took my despair and Mosh's guilt and Jenna's fierce anger and turned it into fucking. The war became my war and my chant was "Fucking bitch, you want it so bad" and I wanted it, too. I raped Mosh in the bathroom like a drunk teenager on a joyride driving down the highway the wrong way at a hundred miles an hour. I became a piece of a machine that worked until it broke without ever knowing why, I fucked her like a demon of vengeance punishing the guilty in hell. Our war would never end, anyway, even if the real war did. I loved her so hard because she was soft and breakable. I loved the way she had a car and a two-room apartment to herself. I wanted to fuck her so hard that it would protect her from ever being fucked over, like a force field of fucking that didn't care how it got where it got, a joy that came out of bitterness. Everything I was afraid someone might do to us: I wanted to do that.

Jenna leaned down to kiss me. She bit my lips so hard I could smell my own blood. And I didn't care that it wasn't safe, because I loved her death wish so much it was almost mine. That little bit of blood was a small thing to worry about compared to a war.

THE LAST SOCIALIST

PETER ORNER

This was in Raleigh during the drought of '93. We lived across the street from a Buick dealer and I'd lie for hours on the couch on the porch and watch the new cars gleam in the sun. My Firenza didn't gleam. She'd come home from a run and be appalled by my idleness all over again. By the end of us, September, she'd stopped bothering to be disgusted.

I remember. She'd stand and hold open the door with one hand and take her shoes off with the other. Her face bright red, her neck, her hair sweat-stuck to her ears. How can you just lie there, all day every day? The only activity I hadn't given up hope on was sex. But even for this it was too hot in Raleigh. One night, at three in the morning, we went to an IHOP because of the air conditioning and she gave me a merciful hand job using the oil from the vinegar-and-oil rack on the table.

Another night, the sweat pooling in the hollow of our mattress, I said, "I could lie beside you like a Sunday roast."

"Where'd you steal that line from?"

"I forget."

She raised her head and kissed me daintily as a small reward. For stealing? For forgetting? Then she fell asleep. The overhead light was on. She said she needed it on to read. She always brought a small tower of books with her to bed. She said she was only studying political science as precursor to overthrow. I stood up on the bed and yanked the cord.

"What are you doing? I'm reading."

"You're not reading. You're sleeping."

"Turn it back on."

I stood back up and yanked the cord again. Then she quoted, without opening her eyes, from the book she'd been reading. "Power cannot be looked forward to or else it is looked forward to indefinitely." Sartre quoting Marx. It was too fucking hot to respond.

"I love you," I said.

"*Vera Zassolich*," she cried to the ceiling.

"What?"

"Vera Zassolich. In 1876 she shot General Trepov after the trial of the hundred and eighty-three populists."

"Killed him?"

"Maimed, but good enough. Not sixteen and she started a revolution. Viva!"

"Viva," I said.

"Fuck me," she said. "Fuck me like a hero."

"Like a proletarian hero?"

"Yes. And then go. Will you?"

"Tonight?"

"Tonight, tomorrow, next week. Just go."

She was naked. I was naked save for my hat. If we could have torn off our skins we would have. I wish I could report the exultancy of the rapturous upheaval. But even in my memory we're like two wet seals thumping. We kept losing our grip on our slippery asses. Two and half minutes, tops. She groaned and rolled off me. She said, "You're no Daniel Ortega." Went back to reading.

Later she got up and took a shower. I stared at the bulb above the bed and listened. We had very low water pressure that summer. All of Raleigh did, according to the *News and Observer*. I stared at the bulb and thought of the water slowly landing on her, slinking down her neck, her shoulders, her breasts, leaping off her pistol nipples into the abyss of the drain.

MY MOST MEMORABLE ENCOUNTER

SUSAN O'DOHERTY

My friend Sherina says I don't know how to act or dress since I don't have a mother, but she is wrong about that. I have had more mothers than most. There is the one that everyone calls my "real" mother, but she doesn't feel real to me because we don't know where she is. My sister, Maura, thinks our "real" mother is coming back for us, but Maura has many problems and this isn't her story. Then there is the mother I have now, Mamie Slattery, who actually counts twice because she gave us back to the agency after Maura set the fire, but now I'm hers again. In between we had Mama Julie, where Maura still stays.

Even so, Sherina is right, I'm not good at girl things. I do have lots of girl friends, mostly because I'm good in school and don't mind giving the answers away. My friends try to help me with dressing and what to say to boys, but it's never exactly right. With clothes, either I'm too dressy or too sloppy, or I mix styles that everyone knows don't go together; and with boys I either can't think of anything to say or I can't stop talking, showing myself in an unattractive light.

One day in the cafeteria Rita told us her aunt Angie was having a party with some fabulous guys and she could get one or two of us invited. Angie is a legend with us. She is ten years younger than Rita's mom and more like a fabulous cousin than an aunt. Her boyfriend drives a Lincoln Town Car for Nicholas Fratelli, the city councilman! As you can imagine, Angie and Dennis go with a very with-it, political crowd. Angie has taken two Martha Stewart entertaining seminars and the councilman himself comes to her parties.

Sherina said, "Ask Katie, she needs to meet a fabulous guy," and everybody laughed, even me. But then Simone said she thought Rita really should invite me. We explained that the Slatterys are very strict and would never let me go to a grown-up boy-girl party even if I did know how to act. Simone's family moved here from Manhattan, so in some ways she's the coolest, and everyone listens to her, but she doesn't understand how things are done in Brooklyn and keeps needing to be filled in.

Rita said that actually the strictness wasn't a problem because we could tell the Slatterys we were sleeping over at Angie's and just skip over the party. That would cover both of us because Rita's mom didn't know about the party either. Even though Rita's mother is Angie's sister there are lots of things she doesn't know. But there was still the problem of my being a complete dork.

Simone said we should make it a project to get me a date with the best guy at the party. Then Sherina said they could do a make-over like on TV, using mainly Simone's clothes and makeup and so on. I'm fatter than Simone, but she has good accessories. Simone said okay, and also that she would teach me things like kissing and touching. Simone goes both ways; maybe it's the Manhattan thing. If a Brooklyn girl slept around she would be a ho, but Simone is not a ho. I said, no, thanks, I don't like girls that way. Simone said that was even better, because if your first time is with somebody you're hot for, you only think about making them like you back, and you should know what makes you feel good. But the rest said, "Eeugh," so she dropped it.

The afternoon of the party, I wore my regular clothes to Rita's and just brought my nightgown, toiletry kit, and clean underwear. Rita's mom drove us to her aunt's and visited for a while. Then, around six o'clock, Sherina, Simone, and Lena came over and we got to work. We used Angie's roommate's bedroom, where Rita and I were going to sleep because the roommate was staying with her boyfriend. Lena is more my size, so she brought some tops. (They said my own jeans were okay.) The group decided on a black spandex tube that we didn't even have to iron—although it was wrinkled from being crushed in the back of a drawer, hiding from Lena's mother—because it was so tight. I thought it was too small and made me look fat, but Simone said, no, I have great tits and need to show them off. I hadn't known that.

Then they started with the makeup. I am very bad at makeup, besides the fact that I'm not allowed to wear anything but lipstick and blush because my (current) mother is so strict. When I do sneak eyeliner, etc., I end up smearing it and looking scary. Simone had to yell at me to hold my eyes open, but she did a good job making them look big and model-y. Then she put some grease on my hair to tame the frizz. After that, Simone put one of her scarves on me. The others don't wear scarves, but I guess that's the Manhattan thing again. I tried it once but my foster "brother," Kevin, the one who was burned in the fire, said, "What's with the bib?" so I took it off. Simone made it look fashionable, though I couldn't say what the difference was.

When I was done they made me turn around, like a model. They all whistled, then left to see a movie, which is what they had told their mothers they were going out to do, and Rita and Angie ate KFC while we put out the appetizers. They wouldn't let me eat because my lipstick was too perfect. Angie made me a drink of juice and vodka, to relax me, but I had to use a straw.

While they were eating, Dennis came over. He knew me from before, but this time he raised his eyebrows and said hey, hey, and Angie said, don't get any ideas, she's fourteen.

Then the guests started coming. First it was regular guys, Dennis's friends, but then it got quiet, like suddenly nobody could think of anything to say, and I saw that the councilman had come in with three other men. You could tell the other guys were important, too, because they wore better shirts than Dennis and his friends, and also had better haircuts. I can't do these things myself, but I notice them, which is why I trust Simone's taste.

The councilman was smaller and fatter than his pictures, but it was easy to see he was the most important of all. Dennis's friends all wanted to shake his hand, and he told some joke I couldn't hear and everybody laughed for a long time. Imagine my surprise when he came right over to Rita and me, with the three important guys and Dennis and his friends following. He even introduced himself, as if we didn't know who he was! Rita reminded him that she's Angie's niece, and he said, "Oh, right, Roberta," and we laughed. Then he said, "And who's this?" meaning me, and my heart beat so hard I thought it was going to shake the tube top off. Dennis said, "Not this one, Nick. The girls will be here any minute." So they wandered off.

Someone turned up the music so loud I couldn't hear it anymore. Then Rita's boyfriend, Jazz, showed up. Rita isn't allowed to see him because of a drug arrest, so I guess this was the only way they could be together, but they didn't have to rush off and leave me with a roomful of strange men. I wondered when the other girls would get there.

I wanted to practice the listening techniques the girls had taught me, but the men were all talking to each other. Dennis was the only one I knew, so I decided to break the ice with him, even though he was off-limits dating-wise. He and some of his friends were listening to one of the important guys tell a story. I went over and stood next to him. "Hey," he said. He put his arm around me without really looking at me.

I couldn't really follow the story because of the loudness of the music. Some guy had tried to pick the important guy up, but he wasn't mad even though he is not gay. I guess the gay guy was a Democrat, or even a Green, because they all thought it was pretty funny and they were happy that they had something now. One of the other important guys walked by our group, talking on a cell phone. He rolled his eyes at our important guy. Ours gave him the finger. Dennis put his drink to my lips and tipped it up so I chugged it. It tasted like soap mixed with dirt, but I figured sharing it counted as flirting, so I just smiled. One of his friends passed him a new drink and we did it again.

The cell phone guy walked by again. He said, yeah, you love that story, Caruso. Too bad it didn't go down like that.

Our guy, Caruso, said, "Fuck you, Flanagan. Too bad you weren't there to make it really go down." He looked at our group to see if we got the joke. I laughed, but more to make him feel better for having his story spoiled. It wasn't that funny, even to someone like me, who is slow to get sex jokes. Caruso looked at us like we were morons and went off for another drink.

As soon as he was gone, Dennis took over as the important person of our group, still with his arm around me. He explained that Caruso and Flanagan hated each other, as if we couldn't tell. "Nick and Caruso go way back," he said. "Now Nick brings in a *media coordinator* and Mike's stuck keeping the books. I'd be pissed, too." One of the other regular guys asked if that meant the rumors were true about Fratelli making a run for the state senate. Dennis gave a look like, wouldn't you like to know. Looking back, now that Fratelli is in the race, it's exciting to think I was there when it was all happening.

Dennis let his hand slip down off my shoulder onto my left boob. I knew that was my cue to say something flirty but I was in that blank state I talked about before, where I can't think of anything to say, and with the music and the drinks it was hard to think. Finally I said, "Simone says I have great tits," which sounds stupid now, but at the time it felt brilliant. Dennis said, "What?" so I shouted it, and all the guys turned to look.

Dennis said, "Those aren't real, though," and I said, "Sure they are." And he said, "Couldn't be, they're too perfect." I said,

"Want to bet?" All of this shouting, because of the music. So Dennis said, "Only one way to find out," and he grabbed the left one hard, like he was trying to pop it. I bruise easily, but he was just being friendly. "Hey, they are real," he said. So then the other guys had to feel, too, all of us laughing. Even Nick, I guess I can call him that, came over to see what the fun was about, and he had a feel, too. "Very, very nice," he said.

That's when Angie came out of the kitchen, looking mad. "Just joking around," Dennis said, but she made him go into her bedroom with her and shut the door.

Nick said it looked like the girls weren't going to show, and who wanted to head over to Diamante's? Of course everyone said yes, so that was the end of the party. One of Dennis's friends turned the music off and we could hear Angie yelling through the bedroom door. Nick gave a nod, and they started moving off.

Caruso asked me if I wanted to come. That's all I needed, to get carded at a strip club. I said no, I was sleeping over tonight. He said, great, me, too. I said, no, really, Angie is Rita's aunt. He said, yeah, she's my aunt, too. It's a pajama party. The other guys laughed. I forgot all the listening techniques and started telling them how Rita and I lied to our moms to get there, and about the makeover and all. The other guys said good luck to Caruso, and they left.

Even though he had a good shirt and haircut, up close Caruso was not that attractive. He was at least thirty, and he smelled like old sweat and cigarette smoke. I guess I wouldn't have made him media coordinator, either, if that means working with media personalities such as Katie Couric (not that I've ever smelled her, but she's very well groomed and would think badly of Nick if he sent over a smelly coordinator).

Caruso started kissing me, and I decided it would be good practice, since I was already loosened up and all, and remembering what Simone said about starting with somebody you aren't hot for.

Then he shoved his tongue down so far I couldn't breathe, and he started ripping at my top. I pulled away and said, "Quit it." He just laughed and started up again. I said it louder. "Quit it," and he said, okay, okay, you sure acted like you wanted it, far be it from me to push myself. He said, believe me, there are plenty who do if you don't.

I waited for him to leave and catch up with his friends, but he poured another drink and slumped down on the couch. In the background we could hear Angie's bed banging up and down. She yelled, "Oh, God," and Dennis was yelling something I couldn't hear. "McGinty got lucky, anyway," he said.

I felt bad for him. First he got stuck keeping the books, whatever that was, then Flanagan ruined his story, and now I had hurt his feelings. "I think keeping the books is a very important position," I said.

"Yeah, I can see you're an expert."

Okay, fine, I thought. "I'm going to bed now. It was nice to meet you," I said.

"Sure, goodnight," he said. "Don't worry about Mike Caruso, honey. Mike Caruso always lands on his feet. Nick don't want me, no problem. I knew a few things about that pansy Flanagan. Mike Caruso is pretty valuable property in this district."

I wondered if that meant he was going over to the Greens, but I decided not to get into it. I went into the roommate's bedroom and shut the door. I was unpacking my overnight case when he came in. I was sorry my attempt to cheer him up didn't work out, but I had no intention of starting up again. "I said I don't want to have sex," I told him.

Hey, he said, who said anything about sex? Just spending the night at my aunt's house with my new friend. Nothing wrong with that, is there?

I had nothing to say to that. I didn't want to walk in on Angie and Dennis, and there was nobody else to tell. He took his pants off. "I told you no," I said, and he said, I don't even want to have sex with you. You're a dog. I'm going to sleep and I'm not putting on some pansy pajamas because some little girl doesn't want to look at a man's equipment. But his thing was all big so I knew he was lying.

Okay, I have to do a flashback now. Our "real" mother lived with an asshole named Ed who used to come in and bother my sister, Maura, and then me. It wasn't real sex, just pushing up against us with our pajamas on, and me only a few times before Maura blew the whistle and got us kicked out. But it was enough so I knew he was hot for me.

I didn't know what to do, and I wished I could have asked Simone, but who knew a situation like this could arise? So, I decided to just act normal. I took my overnight bag into the bathroom and changed into my nightgown, which (this is the part Sherina thinks is hilarious) had little puppies and kittens on it, and brushed my teeth and washed my hands and face, then went back to the bed. "I'm just sleeping, though," I told him, and he said, fine, that's all I want to do.

So I curled up as close to the edge of the bed as possible and tried to act like I was asleep, but I couldn't remember what a sleeping person looks or sounds like. I did remember that Maura used to breathe very loud, almost like snoring, but I was afraid if I did that he'd think it was heavy breathing and come after me again. I decided to just lie there as quiet as I could. After a while, he pulled me over to him and lifted up my nightgown. I started to say no, but he slapped me in the face and said, "Shut up, you know you want it," and before I could think, he was pushing it into me.

When Ed used to do that thing, I learned how to pretend I was floating near the ceiling, watching all this happen to somebody else, that there was no pain and it was even a bit amusing when you looked at it the right way. That's how I was able to be a normal girl the rest of the time, well, not normal in terms of being able to talk to boys, but not going crazy, either. So that's what I did, and it wasn't that bad, and when it was over he even said, that wasn't so bad, was it? And I had to admit it wasn't. Then he went home and I was able to really go to sleep.

The other part Sherina thinks is funny is that the next day he called Angie for my phone number, and Angie had to tell him I'm only fourteen and he'd better not try and track me down. Which he never did. So I didn't actually get a boyfriend out of it, but it did improve my popularity, both because I proved that I can look good enough to get a grown man, a political figure, interested in me, and because it really does make a good story, doesn't it? Even I have to laugh at the nightgown part. Except the one time we got into Lena's parents' liquor cabinet and they made me tell it to Lena's sister, and when I got to that part, instead of laughing I started crying and couldn't stop, and then I threw up. Other than that, though, it's okay. But I wish I had let Simone be first.

THE TRUE REPUBLIC

STEVE ALMOND

Everyone always said the truly freaky shit happened down in the Republic, but I never believed them. I figured it was gossip, the natural oxygen of a bullshit nation. What I knew of the Republic was what I saw on TV: rioting around the petroleum islands, the roving water militias, the lavish, fortified estates where leaders played golf and decided which sector would get the next nuclear plant.

I was a typical New American, I guess: earnest, vaguely patriotic, vegetarian. I had grown up in Vermont Province. I was still in junior high when the Great Line was drawn. My parents supported the referendum. They could see where things were headed. A house divided and all that.

I'd visited the Republic only once, in high school, but that was before China called in their chits and everything went apeshit. You could still travel without an escort then. The roads were cracking, and I remember seeing a few work camps around the capital. They told us those were collective farms.

My cousin Clem had visited back in '28, on one of those corporate Desalinization Fellowships. The whole thing wigged him out. The armored vehicles, the drug tests, the prayer circle debriefings—not his scene.

We all wanted to know about quality-of-life stuff.

Clem shook his head.

"Fried food and pig shit, man."

That was his executive summary.

So I had no intention of seeing the Republic again. But, then, I never meant to sign on with the Sticky Icky Dirt Band, either. Just sort of fell into it. They needed someone to run the light board and electronic effects. I needed a winter job to supplement my soybean crop.

The Sticky Icky was a trio of college burnouts who did trance-hop covers of cheesy oldies: Depeche Mode, Nine Inch Nails. I doubted they would stay together long enough to grow out their dreadlocks. Certainly none of us expected that our lone single, "Unchain Your Brain," would become a hit down south.

"Fucking racist pigs," said Phred, our lead singer. He was half Vietnamese, half trust-fund.

Nonetheless, one day we found ourselves in receipt of a certified letter from Mr. Shivalik Khan, one of the young Saudis who had bought up most of the Gulf's swamps. He wanted us to play his twenty-first-birthday bash, at the beachfront arena in Orlando. A forty-five-minute gig for five hundred thousand rands. Enclosed was a check for a hundred thousand rands.

The show was a disaster. Most of our equipment ran off a solar grid, not generators. Our bassist, Tork, kept smacking up against the bulletproof barrier. But the crowd was so cranked on Bliss tabs it didn't even matter.

Khan stood in the royal box, in a long blue robe, and did his jerky Arab noodle dance. An older woman, presumably his mother, sat beside him, bored out of her skull.

After the show, we got loaded onto a copter and whisked off to his compound. We set down on this parapet and looked down across a thick lawn, to the lagoon with the waterslide, the Aruban sand strobing blue, two full bars, giant, freshwater Jacuzzi, steam room, sauna. And scattered across all of this: naked betties, laughing, smacking each other on the butt, swilling mai tais.

"Holy crap," Tork said.

"Totally unmonitored," Khan said. "Fuck anything you see."

"Have they been tested?" Phred said.

Khan let out a peal of girlish laughter. "You poor little sodbuster. They're virgins. Certified." He spread his arms. "Welcome to the fruits of repression."

We were all young guys, horny enough, but we were New Americans, subject to certain sensitivities.

"They're, what, fucking fourteen?" said Hankhank, our drummer. "I'm not busting some underage hymen."

Tork shrugged.

Khan fed us vodka tonics, Bliss tabs, some smoke. The drinks had been dosed with enhancers, naturally, and the blood rushed straight to our dongs.

The girls descended on us. They were way out of our league: pale Slavs, tall Africans, Peruvian sex bombs dipped in balsam. They laughed at everything we said and stripped the clothing from our bodies and pulled us to the ground and shouted things that our girls never said, in these ridiculous accents:

"Let me lick-lick!"

"Put in ass, put *hard!*"

"Squirt the face now!"

They took our hands and placed them around their throats.

We were all hopped up on stimulants; they made us fierce, predatory, unable to quell our erections.

"You like that tight little cave?" my third girl said. She was Inuit, I believe. "Bust that bitch in two so I can suck the blood off."

Khan watched all of this from his perch. He could see the expressions on our faces, our savage porno sneers. It gave him great pleasure to watch us break free of the polite gender politics we'd absorbed up north.

I heard someone calling my name, a girl down the beach lolling under a palm tree. I staggered toward her. She stepped from the shadows, and my chest seized up.

"It can't be," I said.

Tork, behind me, said, "Good Christ. It is. Jenna fucking Bush."

We all remembered her from the memorial video in our safety training classes. She'd been kidnapped by diesel bikers during the

2012 Texas blackout and found a few months later, in parts. But she was alive now, restored to her sorority girl prime, an image I had jacked off to countless times as a pimpled teen. She stood luxurious in her rolls of baby fat, with her twat shaved down to a tender pink pucker.

"Who all is going to fuck this nasty cunt?" she said, in her soft drawl. "This nasty, horny cunt?"

I turned and spotted Khan. He grinned broadly.

"Jesus," I said. "She's a synthetic."

Tork nodded. He was watching Doris Day eat out Paris Hilton. Then we caught sight of Hankhank. He was tittie-fucking a young Marilyn Monroe on the dock, while Betty Page licked his ass.

At a certain point, a loudspeaker came on and beckoned us to the amphitheater. Klieg lights washed down onto a steel cage, inside of which two naked men circled each other. They had cocks like thick hammers—obvious products of the Genital Enhancement Program—and they went at one another with a merciless, dead-eyed hunger.

We'd heard about such things: Ultimate Fag Fighting, it was called. The winners were allowed to sodomize the loser—to death, if they so chose.

I turned away, stumbled off to a high bluff. The bodies below had assumed a frantic, tribal rhythm. I could pick out particular images: a little redhead at the edge of the lagoon, impaled by giants on either end, held aloft, bucking, gagging on a third. A black woman in congress with a sullen Shetland pony. A pair of crew-cut club boys writhing in a pool of semen.

The whole thing was so fucking out of hand. It was like a Bosch painting, and impossible to look away.

"You like the sick shit, huh?" Khan said.

I must have nodded, because I was led by the hand to a dank grotto. In one vestibule, we watched a priest calmly insert his meaty fist into a bucket of lard, then into a series of effeminate altar boys.

"Catamites," Khan said. "Quite wrong for them to be alive."

In the next, a scowling mother superior introduced a pack of frightened novitiates to the rigors of genital mutilation. The noises of the victims were amplified and run through an echo effect.

The drugs made it hard for me to react to all this properly. But I managed to convey some basic brand of distress to Khan.

"Don't you see?" he said mildly. "They choose to come here. It is a paradise for them, to feel these things. They will be stars forever."

It turned out the entire compound was rigged with cameras. Khan was livestreaming. We were merely a minor attraction—a one-hit band from the other side—to supplement the various star athletes, synthetics, homosexuals, and several hundred cock-starved virgins. All entirely illegal under the Moral Code of the Republic.

He made a fortune off the downloads, particularly those that included the special snuff featurette. The political leadership was happy to collect kickbacks. Khan had a hidden archive with most of them on film, just in case.

It was the only durable economy, he explained. With the crude almost gone and the aquifers sucked dry, porn had become the last, best resort for most citizens. They would spend a few months on the compound, then be shipped west and dumped in the desert provinces. They understood that.

"Without me, they have what? Prayer and starvation," Khan said. "I only give them what they've always wanted." He smiled a thin smile. "And, you know, I do pledge allegiance—every day: to the Republic and that for which it stands."

CONTRIBUTORS

STEVE ALMOND is the author of two story collections, *My Life in Heavy Metal* and *The Evil B. B. Chow*. His collection of essays, *Not That You Asked*, was published in 2007 by Random House. He lives outside Boston with his wife and new baby daughter, whom he cannot stop kissing.

JONATHAN AMES is the author of *I Pass Like Night*, *The Extra Man*, *What's Not to Love?*, *My Less Than Secret Life*, *Wake Up, Sir!*, and *I Love You More Than You Know*. His graphic novel, *The Alcoholic*, will be published in 2008 by DC Comics/Vertigo. He is the editor of the anthology *Sexual Metamorphosis* and the winner of a Guggenheim Fellowship. For more information, see his Web site: www.jonathanames.com.

CHARLIE ANDERS is the author of *Choir Boy*, which won a Lambda Literary Award. She co-edited the anthology *She's Such a Geek: Women Write About Science, Technology, and Other Nerdy Stuff*. She also publishes *Other* magazine and organizes the Writers with Drinks reading series. She likes to role-play that she lives in a democracy. "Transfixed, Helpless, and Out of Control: Election Night 2004" was originally published in Suspect Thoughts Online.

JAMI ATTENBERG is the author of the short story collection *Instant Love* and the novel *The Kept Man*. Her fiction and nonfiction have appeared in *Print*, Nerve, Salon, *Nylon, Jane, Pindeldyboz, Spork,* the *San Francisco Chronicle*, and elsewhere. Visit her online at www.jamiatten berg.com.

NICK FLYNN's book *Another Bullshit Night in Suck City* (Norton, 2004) won the PEN/Martha Albrand Award for First Nonfiction, was shortlisted for France's Prix Femina, and has been translated into thirteen languages. He is also the author of two books of poetry, *Some Ether* (Graywolf, 2000) and *Blind Huber* (Graywolf, 2002), for which he received fellowships from, among other organizations, the Guggenheim Foundation and the Library of Congress. Some of the venues his poems, essays, and nonfiction have appeared in include *The New Yorker, The Paris Review,* National Public Radio's *This American Life,* and the *New York Times Book Review.* His film credits include "field poet" and artistic collaborator on the film *Darwin's Nightmare,* which was nominated for an Academy Award for Best Feature Documentary in 2006. One semester a year he teaches at the University of Houston, and he then spends the rest of the year elsewhere.

JAMES FREY is originally from Cleveland. He lives in New York.

AVITAL GAD-CYKMAN is the author of stories published in *McSwee-ney's*, *Michigan Quarterly Review*, *Other Voices*, *Glimmer Train*, *Prism International*, and anthologies such as *Stumbling and Raging*. She lives on an island in Brazil and hopes to publish a collection and a novel soon.

DAPHNE GOTTLIEB is the author and/or editor of six books of poetry and fiction, most recently *Kissing Dead Girls*. She lives in San Francisco, where she teaches at New College of California.

LIZ HENRY is a blogger, literary critic, poet, translator, and geek. She is a contributing editor for BlogHer.org. You can find her online at www.bookmaniac.net. "Capitol Punishment" was originally published in *Suspect Thoughts: A Journal of Subversive Writing*.

KEITH KNIGHT is an award-winning cartoonist and rapper whose two weekly comic strips, *the K Chronicles and (th)ink,* can be found in more than thirty-five alternative weekly, ethnic, political, and college publica-tions nationwide. He is also a regular contributor to *MAD* and *ESPN the Magazine*. His semiconscious hip-hop band, the Marginal Prophets, will kick your ass. His new *(th)ink* collection, *Are We Feeling Safer Yet?*, can be seen at www.kchronicles.com.

TSAURAH LITZKY believes the only thing left that might take Amer-ica collectively higher is increased appreciation of the joys of sex. This inspires her to keep writing raunchy stories. Her erotica has appeared in more than sixty-five publications. Simon & Schuster published her erotic novella, *The Motion of the Ocean*, as part of *Three the Hard Way*, a series of erotic novellas edited by Susie Bright. Litzky's prize-winning course, *Silk Sheets: Writing Erotica*, is now in its ninth year at the New School in Manhattan.

LYDIA MILLET is the author of six novels, most recent *How the Dead Dream* (2008), *Oh Pure and Radiant Heart* (2007), which was short-listed for Britain's Arthur C. Clarke Prize. Her 2002 novel, *My Happy Life*, won the PEN/USA Award for Fiction. She is also an essayist and critic and works as an editor at the nonprofit Center for Biological Diversity.

RICK MOODY's most recent publications are *The Diviners* (2005), a novel, and *Right Livelihoods* (2007), a collection of three novellas. "Notes on Redevelopment" was first published, in a somewhat different form, on Nerve.com in 2006.

MISTRESS MORGANA is an experienced San Francisco–based BDSM professional and sex educator. Her workshops on BDSM have delighted thousand of kink-curious people of all persuasions, and she is the co-writer and host of the instructional video *Whipsmart: A Good Vibrations Guide to SM for Beginning Couples*. Her writing has appeared in *The Best American Erotica 2005* and *Politically Inspired*. Mistress Morgana believes that the current Bush administration is neither safe, sane, nor consensual and could learn a great deal from the ethics of BDSM play.

VANESSA NORTON was born and raised in Buffalo, New York. She has worked as a dietary aide in a nursing home, a waitress, a teacher, a house cleaner, a labor organizer, a puppeteer, a stripper, a bookstore clerk, and a vote canvasser. She currently resides in Eugene, Oregon, where she is completing her MFA in fiction at the University of Oregon.

SUSAN O'DOHERTY is a writer and clinical psychologist who lives in Brooklyn, New York. She is the author of *Getting Unstuck Without Coming Unglued: A Woman's Guide to Unblocking Creativity* (Seal Press, 2007). Her popular advice column for writers, "The Doctor Is In," appears every Friday on MJ Rose's publishing blog, Buzz, Balls, & Hype. Her stories, poems, and essays have appeared in *Eureka Literary Magazine, Northwest Review, Apalachee Review,* and the anthologies *About What Was Lost: Twenty Writers on Miscarriage, Healing, and Hope* (Penguin, 2007) and *It's a Boy!* (Seal Press, 2005). Her story "Passing" was chosen as the New York story for Ballyhoo Stories' ongoing *Fifty States Project* and will be distributed in chapbook form in bookstores throughout New York State.

ERIC ORNER is a cartoonist and animation artist whose comics and graphic short stories have appeared in *Newsweek, The New Republic,* and *McSweeney's.* He has worked on a number of animated productions, including a stint as an artist on Disney's upcoming *Tinker Bell* movie. A feature film based on Eric's widely syndicated alt-weekly comic strip, *The Mostly Unfabulous Social Life of Ethan Green,* was released nationally in 2006. The comic strip has been anthologized in four books from St. Martin's Press.

PETER ORNER is the author of the novel *The Second Coming of Mavala Shikongo* (finalist for the Los Angeles Times Book Prize), and the story collection *Esther Stories* (recipient of the Rome Fellowship from the American Academy of Arts and Letters). He has been awarded fellowships from the Lannan and Guggenheim foundations. Orner lives in San Francisco.

MICHELLE RICHMOND is the author, most recently, of *The Year of Fog.* Her stories and essays have appeared in *Playboy, Glimmer Train, The*

Missouri Review, Salon.com, *The Kenyon Review*, and elsewhere. She lives in San Francisco and publishes the online literary journal Fiction Attic.

JERRY STAHL has written a number of books, including *Permanent Midnight* and *I, Fatty.* "Li'l Dickens" originally appeared in his short story collection *Love Without.*

ANTHONY SWOFFORD is the author of the memoir *Jarhead* (Scribner, 2003). A film adaptation directed by Sam Mendes was released in 2005. His novel *Exit A* (Scribner) was published in January of 2007. His writing has appeared in *Harper's*, the *New York Times*, the *New York Times Magazine*, *The Guardian*, and *The Telegraph Magazine*, among other places. He has taught at St. Mary's College, Lewis and Clark College, and the Iowa Writers' Workshop. His awards include the PEN Art of the Memoir award, for *Jarhead*, and a James Michener/Copernicus Society Fiction Fellowship. He lives in New York City, where he is at work on a new novel. "Escape and Evasion" was originally published in *ZYZZYVA.*

MICHELLE TEA is the editor of four anthologies and the author of four memoirs, one collection of poetry, and the novel *Rose of No Man's Land.* She runs Radar Productions, a literary nonprofit that stages performance events in San Francisco and elsewhere.

Called a "trollop with a laptop" by the *East Bay Express* and a "literary siren" by Good Vibrations, **ALISON TYLER** is naughty and she knows it. Her sultry short stories have appeared in more than seventy anthologies, including *Sweet Life* (Cleis), *Sex at the Office* (Virgin), and *Glam-*

our Girls (Alyson). She is the author of more than twenty-five erotic novels and the editor of more than thirty explicit anthologies, including *A Is for Amour, B Is for Bondage, C Is for Co-Eds,* and *D Is for Dress-up* (all just out from Cleis). Please visit www.alisontyler.com for more information.